Praise for *The Four Profound Weaves*

"*The Four Profound Weaves* is a balm and a call to arms. R. B. Lemberg reassures us that there's still time to find yourself, no matter how old you are; and they stir our revolutionary urges to defeat murderous dictators . . . Thoughtful and deeply moving, *The Four Profound Weaves* is the anti-authoritarian, queer-mystical fairy tale we need right now."

—Annalee Newitz, author of *The Future of Another Timeline*

★"DEBUT. Nebula-nominated Lemberg's first novella, set in their deeply queer "Birdverse" universe, presents a beautiful, heartfelt story of change, family, identity, and courage. Centering two older transgender protagonists in the midst of emotional and physical journeys highlights the deep, meaningful prose that Lemberg always brings to their stories."

—*Library Journal*, starred review

★"Lemberg writes deeply considered, evocative portraits of their characters, handling sexuality and gender especially well. This diverse, folkloric fantasy world is a delight to visit.

—*Publishers Weekly*, starred review

★"R. B. Lemberg spins a world of singing gods, desert nomads, and magic humming in the wind in *The Four Profound Weaves* . . . Impressive world building renders the shifting hues of the desert sands and the cold stone of The Collector's palace in tight prose."

—*Foreword*, starred review

"Thought-challenging points-of-view weave together stark violence, intricate powers, and the musings of long and complicated lives. *The Four Profound Weaves* contains imagery that glows on the page."
—Patricia A. McKillip, author of the Riddle-Master Trilogy

"R. B. Lemberg writes with a luminous pen, spraying light all around their words and ideas. They create a universe where carpets and cloaks bear history and the future . . . A complex and mystical journey toward friendship, family, and love."
—Jewelle Gomez, author of *The Gilda Stories*

"R. B. Lemberg's *The Four Profound Weaves* takes the reader on a deeply resonant journey of transformation and strength. Lemberg's lyrical skill, combined with unforgettable characters and the magic of the Birdverse makes a stunning fabric over which this story plays beautifully."
—Fran Wilde, author of The Bone Universe series and The Gemworld series

"Go read this story, tell it to your friends, and help us get to that future that we so desperately need."
—L. A. Lanquist, *Trans Narrative*

"This story, very poetically, holds a mirror to society. It discusses the nuances of the trans experience and made me assess things I hadn't previously known or understood. It has had a profound impact on me."
—*A Bookish Reader*

"In reading this story about recognition and transformation, I felt recognized and transformed. It's fantastic alchemy on

Lemberg's part, and their love and labor shines off the page."
—Nino Cipri, author of *Homesick*

"Let this be your introduction to R. B.'s world of song carpets, deepnames, and deserts full of roving lovers."
—Isaac R. Fellman, author of *The Breath of the Sun*

"I am staggered by the richness and intricacy of R. B. Lemberg's imagination. *The Four Profound Weaves* is an intense and emotional story of a journey of change, growth, and courage."
—Kate Elliott, author of *Court of Fives*

"*The Four Profound Weaves* is a jewel-bright tile in [Lemberg's] ongoing mosaic."
—C. S. E. Cooney, author of *Bone Swans, Stories*

"If the plot is the warp of a story, then the weft of this novella is Lemberg's exquisitely crafted, luminescent prose."
—Maria Haskins, author of *Odin's Eye*

"Lemberg weaves a gripping tale of community, identity, betrayal, and hope. From the sweeping expanse of the desert to the confined splendor of a sinister palace, every page contains wonder."
—Julia Rios, Hugo Award-winning editor

"Lyrical and unflinching."
—Rivers Solomon, PEN America

"Sweet and fierce, devastating and gentle in its truths."
—M. Crane Hana, author of *The Purist*

THE FOUR PROFOUND WEAVES
R. B. LEMBERG

Other Books by R. B. Lemberg

Poetry
Marginalia to Stone Bird (2016)

As Editor:
An Alphabet of Embers (2016)
*Here, We Cross: a collection of queer and
genderfluid poetry from Stone Telling 1–7* (2012)

THE FOUR PROFOUND WEAVES

R. B. LEMBERG

TACHYON
SAN FRANCISCO

The Four Profound Weaves
Copyright © 2020 by R.B. Lemberg

Cover design by Elizabeth Story
Initial concepts by Francesca Myman

Interior design by Elizabeth Story

Tachyon Publications LLC
1459 18th Street #139
San Francisco, CA 94107
www.tachyonpublications.com
tachyon@tachyonpublications.com

Series Editor: Jacob Weisman
Project Editor: Jaymee Goh

Print ISBN 13: 978-1-61696-334-7
Digital formats: 978-1-61696-335-4

First Edition: 2020
9 8 7 6 5 4 3 2 1

To the writers convened by K., A., K., and M.:

for love, survival, and support.

ABOUT THE BIRDVERSE

Dear Readers,

Thank you very much for reading my debut, and welcome to Birdverse!

I began writing in Birdverse back in 2011, when LGBTQIA+ fiction was thin on the ground, and I published a number of short stories and poems. *The Four Profound Weaves* is my first full-length printed book set in Birdverse—everything else is short-form and online.

Birdverse is an LGBTQIA+-focused secondary world with a Bird deity. Few people can see Bird during their lifetime, but everybody sees her when they die: she comes for the souls of the dead in the shape of a bird most dear to each person—a finch, a plover, a mythical harptail, a firebird.

You don't have to have any background in Birdverse to read this book.

My storytelling in Birdverse to date is kind of circular—there is no beginning or end to it. If you are curious about my short fiction set in Birdverse, I recommend these three stories: "The Desert Glassmaker and the Jeweler of Berevyar" in *Uncanny Magazine*, which is a short epistolary romance between two artists; "Grandmother-nai-Leylit's Cloth of Winds," a Nebula Award finalist, in *Beneath Ceaseless Skies*, the story of the cloth of winds and the precursor to this novella; and "Geometries of Belonging," also in *Beneath Ceaseless Skies*, about a depressed queer mind-healer who refuses to "cure" a young autistic patient. These stories can be found by searching their titles online.

Happy reading!

R. B. Lemberg
September 2020

I.
CHANGE

THE
SNAKE-SURUN'
ENCAMPMENT

Uiziya e Lali

I sat alone in my old goatskin tent. Waiting, like I had for the last forty years, for Aunt Benesret to come back. Waiting to inherit her loom and her craft, the mastery of the Four Profound Weaves. I wasn't sure how long I'd been sitting like this, and it was dark in the tent; I no longer knew day from night.

When the faded red woven tapestry at the entrance shifted aside, I drew my breath sharply, waiting for my aunt's thin, almost skeletal hand—but it was not Benesret. Of course not. Instead, one of my grand-nieces stepped in, plump and full of life, bedecked in embroideries and circlets hammered with snakes. Her eyes shone like stars in the gloom.

"Aunt Uiziya, don't sit here alone. Aunt Uiziya, you should come to the trading tent. Aunt Uiziya, bring some of these weaves—" The girl's bejeweled hand motioned at the weavings that hung, heavy and lifeless, around my tent. "You might sell something, and if not, just show your craft, yes?" And just like a flutter of wind, she was gone.

I kept sitting. But something had changed, as if some sliver of song entered my dead domain and withdrew. I had woven so much in those decades of waiting for my aunt to come back, but I wouldn't show them. None of them sang and yearned like hers did, none of them called the goddess Bird down from the merciless heat of the sky. My weaves hung lifeless, like bodies. Who would want them? Did I want them? I had not thought about that, just sat among them, the guardian of all the unwanted, forgotten things. I turned sixty-three this year; I would sit like this, until I sat among bones. My aunt could weave even from bones, but she never finished teaching me.

The flap of my tent had not been fully closed, and now the riot of light and of sounds trickled in, only half-real to my senses after a day spent in gloom. It was the commotion of trading—the rustling of cloth, the heavy sound of carpets unrolled for display, the bleating of goats. So much excitement in the encampment—the traders must be foreign. Show my craft? What craft? My life had stopped, like a wind trapped in a fist.

I'll make a weaver out of you yet, my aunt Benesret had said to me. *I'll teach you—I'll teach you, just wait. I'll teach you the Four Profound Weaves so that you will inherit my loom.*

Where was she, then? Where was she? The guardian snakes that circumnavigated the encampment all knew her, and I doubted she would be allowed to enter, but she could have tried, at least. She could have sent me a letter. She could have sent an assassin, one of those she worked with, to kill the snakes and find me and bring me to her.

The girl should have left me alone, but now I was angry and hot and I wanted . . . I wanted something that wasn't this endless wait. Show my craft, like it once was, all the promise of the desert and its secret weaves, endless future that never came to be.

I was too large and too old for rash movements, but I dragged myself up, stiff in my joints from being still for so long. Hesitantly, I unlatched a large chest of leather in which I kept especially precious things. My late husband's wedding shirt, embroidered by my own hands before they wrinkled. A small ball of spidersilk spun by my daughter when she was a little girl. A note from the nameless man before he became nameless, given to me forty years ago. Beneath the precious debris of my life, a rustle of sand.

At last I pulled the thin, rolled-up carpet, hidden away these forty years. Shook it out. It was as long as I was tall, and slightly shorter in width. Sand grains made its threads, yellow and dun and shadow-warmth; thread-bones peeked out of their hiding places in the weave. If I called on my magical deep-names, I could make the carpet of sand float and fly, all the way up to the guardian poles of the tent.

Show your craft. You might even sell it.

"I have a carpet for sale," I said to no one in particular. "A carpet woven from sand, the second of the Four Profound Weaves that Aunt Benesret taught me before she was exiled." This carpet, that I had never shown anyone else but her. I would sell it, give it away, even—and then my yearning and my waiting would be done. And I would be done.

the nameless man

Everybody seemed to have gone to the trading tents, and so I made my way there as well. I was hoping to see my grandchildren, always too busy those days to spend time with me. It was true that I did not want to be trading, but if someone was trading, Aviya for sure would be there.

The trading tents were open to the air, supported with carved poles to which the lightweight cloths of the roof attached festive woven ribbons. People milled under these awnings, mostly women—Surun' weavers of all ages, each with a carpet or carpets for sale; and a few of their beloved snakes. The crowd parted as I entered, and in that moment my fears came true.

Three men stood in the middle of the trading tent. They had the gold rods of trade, and gold coins sewn onto the trim of their red felt hats. The men's eyes shone; their dark beards were groomed and oiled, and adorned with the tiniest bells that shook and jingled as they bent over the wares. I sensed powerful magic from all three of them. Their magic—multiple short deepnames—shone in their minds, each deepname like a flaring, spiky star. I was powerful myself, but the strangers' power was that of capturing, of imprisonment, of destruction, held tightly at bay. The vision made me recoil. These men—and it was always men—belonged to the Ruler of Iyar. The Collector.

I had been living here for three months with my grandchildren, among our friends the snake-Surun'. Almost three months after my transformation, my ceremony of change. I thought I had finally broken free from Iyar. But now Iyar came here.

My Surun' friends did not seem to feel any danger. They brought forth carpet after carpet, traditional indigo weaves embroidered with lions, with snakes, with birds, and more modern designs of dyed madder and bold geometric shapes. The Iyari traders examined the offerings one by one yet chose nothing, their faces still with masked disgust.

I wanted to shout at my friends to stop this trade. I wanted to run away, to escape unseen. I wanted to fight, to strike at these men, to demand recompense for all the wrongs the Collector inflicted upon me and mine forty years ago.

But then I saw my granddaughter.

Aviya-nai-Bashri was dressed in her trading best— a matching shirt and voluminous pants of green and pink cloth that contrasted so beautifully with her smooth brown skin. Her fish earrings, fashioned of hammered silver, chimed in tune with her words. Her Surun' friends, all girls of nineteen and twenty, milled around, giggling with excitement.

"We offer a carpet of wind," Aviya nai-Bashri all but sang, "A cloth woven of purest wind caught wandering over the desert—a treasure like this you will never see . . ."

The carpet she offered was small and exquisite, made from the tiniest movements of air that come awake, breath after breath, as the dawn tints the desert pink and silver. The threads that made the carpet were delicate flurries of blue not so much woven but whispered into cloth, convinced to come together by the magic of deepnames and laughter.

I'd never seen this weave, but knew who made it. My youngest grandchild. Something like tears welled in my eyes, but I would not allow myself that emotion. I looked around instead, and yes, I saw Kimi, a child of twelve, dancing between two guardian snakes. Kimi laughed, and a flurry of pink butterflies shook themselves loose from the carpet of wind. They sparkled in the air for a moment, then winked out of sight, delicate like my grandchild's magic.

I remembered Uiziya's words, spoken to me before

my ceremony. *The first of the Four Profound Weaves is woven from wind. It signifies change.*

One of the emissaries leaned forward over Kimi's carpet. He pressed a finger to the carpet, and a butterfly rose from it, its wings so delicate I could barely discern the movement of pink against the Iyari man's palm. "What price for this?"

Why did Aviya deal with these men? What was the need, the necessity? We were well supplied from our previous trades, we were doing well and could refuse any trade, especially such a troubling one—what was she doing?

I spoke in my native Khana. "This carpet is not for sale."

"Yes, it is," Aviya said stubbornly.

I grabbed her by the arm, dragged her out from under the awning, carpet and all. She glared at me, defiant, and I did my best to ignore it. "What are you doing?"

"Trading. I'm trading, grandfather, that thing I trained for all my life. You trained me. Before you went through your change."

I grimaced. "This is for the Collector. We did not leave Iyar to trade with him, we left Iyar to never see him again—"

"This is Kimi's first carpet they wove completely alone," Aviya said. "Their first trade. Don't spoil it, grandfather. Please."

"First trade?" I shouldn't have gotten so angry, so

bitter. "The Collector imprisoned your grandmother. Killed her. You want Kimi's first trade to be to this man?"

She propped her fists at her waist and glared at me, half-angry, half-exasperated. "And yours wasn't? Your first trade, your second, your third? The weave of song, the greatest carpet ever woven—you sold it to the Collector!"

"Yes, but there was a reason . . ."

"We are traders, grandfather. Khana women trade. Shouldn't you go sit with the men?"

It would have been better if she'd slapped me.

I turned away. She ran after me, perhaps not wanting to wound me after the spear of her words had already made its way through my chest. "I am sorry, grandfather. I did not mean . . ."

I waited, for a brief moment, for her to say what she meant, but she looked confused—not because she couldn't find a way to speak her mind, I thought, but because my existence, the change, had confused her—had confused and hurt every Khana person who loved me, or so I thought to myself. I had thought about it for forty years before I finally changed my body. I thought how my people judged me, how my lovers Bashri had judged me, how my grandchildren judged me, except perhaps Kimi, who did not know how to judge. Forty years. Even in a woman's body I wanted so desperately to be a man, I *was* a man—and now, a month after my change, in a man's body at last, I did not know how to stop flinching from their judgment. At best, their confusion. Aviya loved me, I knew, but her tongue kept slipping.

"It's fine." It wasn't, but I did not want to talk anymore. It hurt too much to talk, again and again, about the same thing. So I walked away.

Something made me look back. Aviya remained standing by the trading tent, the cloth of winds tucked clumsily under her arm. A stray butterfly followed me, pink and translucent; I reached out to it, but it slipped through my fingers, into the air.

Uiziya e Lali

Everybody seemed to be in the trading tents, but I dragged my feet—and not just because of the pain from sitting still for so long. The encampment felt empty. The carpet of sand on my shoulder whispered into my ear of the wide-open spaces where I wanted and dreaded to go. It was thin, almost weightless, as if it wanted to fly away from my shoulder. I tried to imagine what I would do next, after I traded the carpet away. Sell my tent and my weavings and move to some other encampment, where nobody knew me and nobody gossiped? Walk out into the desert without any water, and wait for the goddess Bird to come for my soul? Go look for that thing that I dreaded? Go back to my tent and sit once again?

I stepped closer and closer, my resolve liquefying like sweat, when I saw my old acquaintance, the nameless man. He was all but running away from the tents, his lighter brown face a grimace of anger-pain-anger I'd come to recognize in him.

Seeing me, he stopped, and averted his gaze.

"What's going on?" I asked.

"Nothing."

A thin green snake slithered in the dusk between us, as if drawing a boundary I should not cross. I stepped right over it.

"So what is going on?" I had a habit of repeating a question until it was answered.

"Go see for yourself," he said. "Trading is a woman's business, I'm told."

"Is it Aviya again? Telling you to go sit with the men?"

"Yes. But there's more—they are selling Kimi's weave." He spoke bitterly. "Like the one you'd all woven for my transformation, but Kimi made it alone, out of joy and wind and—and these butterflies . . ."

I had woven a carpet of change for myself, at the dawn of my life.

"*I will teach you to weave from wind,*" my aunt had said to me then, "*the first mystery of the ever-changing desert. A weave of change: the first of the Four Profound*

Weaves I will teach you until you are ready to put together my loom."

The nameless man spoke on, his voice shaking with the speed and vehemence of his feeling. "My grandchild's first carpet, first trade, to be traded to the Collector, to be held by the Collector's hands, and they all think it's nothing. Joyful even. Joyful!" He took a deep breath. Spoke a bit slower. "What joy is there in trading the cloth of change to a man who will never change? The Collector will lock this cloth in his coffers, away from all eyes but his, away from the people who would use it, who need it, themselves, to change."

I sighed. "Kimi doesn't want to change yet."

"Then she should—he should—they should—" The nameless man waved his hand in exasperation. "Kimi should keep the cloth and transform already!"

"Your grandchild hasn't chosen whether to transform," I said patiently, as I had many times before. "It may never matter to them to go through the change in the body. It is enough that they would weave." I was a good listener, if nothing else; but this I had listened to over and over. The nameless man's people, the Khana, did not recognize in-betweeners. The nameless man's people did not recognize people like him, either; instead, they insisted that the shape of one's body determined one's fate. "The Khana are not the only people in the world who make up these rules and these freedoms."

The nameless man waved his hand in the air again, as if to shoo a stray butterfly. Then he eyed me with a bit more attentiveness. "You, too, bring a carpet to the tent?"

"As you see." I wanted him to ask me about the carpet. I wanted him to ask me why. I wanted to tell him then of my endless waiting, and how I wanted it to be over. I was a good listener, but now I wanted him to listen as I told him about Aunt Benesret. After he came back to us after forty years away, he kept asking about Benesret, and everybody shushed him, because in our encampment we did not say her name.

But he asked me nothing. Just squinted at my carpet and said, "You shouldn't sell it, either."

"How like a man, to tell me what I should and shouldn't do." Half-exasperation, half-compliment in acknowledgment of his change, the words flew out of my mouth before I knew it.

He grimaced bitterly. "That's right. I'll just go sit with the men, then."

Then he walked past me, head drawn into his shoulders.

The Four Profound Weaves

the nameless man

I walked where my feet took me, to the outskirts of the encampment. I thought Uiziya might follow me, but she didn't. I was on my own, and perhaps that was best.

After my transformation, I tried sitting with the Surun' men. They had showed me how to speak Surun' like a man and how to move, how to shave my face Surun'-style. They were friends and good people, but I did not want to go much deeper into their ways. I was no warrior. I could fight when I needed, but that was not what being a man meant to me. I wasn't Surun'. I was Khana.

Our people lived in Iyar, but we weren't Iyari. Behind the walls of our quarter, walled off from the rest of the city by royal decrees, the Khana lived separate lives, and in the Khana quarter, women and men lived separate lives yet again, divided from each other by an inner wall.

Our men were scholars, not warriors. Scholars and makers of magical automata for the utter glory of Bird and her hidden brother, the singer Kimri. As a child I would wake up in darkness to stand under the white walls of the men's inner quarter, where I wasn't allowed—waiting—waiting for our men to sing the dawnsong to bring the sibling gods closer, and with them, the dawn.

But now I was here, far east and away from Iyar,

in the great Burri desert. It was here, at this very place, in this dust, on the outskirts of the snake-Surun' encampment, I had stood in my cloth made of winds, the weave of transformation my friends and my grandchildren had woven for me out of love. I'd lifted my arms to the sky and the sandbirds had come to me, sent to me by the goddess Bird and summoned by the cloth of winds. They were birds of bright fire that fell from the sky and cocooned me, until I could see and hear nothing except the warmth and the feathers enveloping me and the threads of the wind singing each to each until my whole skin was ignited by the sun, my body changing and changed by the malleable flame. And when it was done, I sang.

I sang as the wind and the feathers dissolved into sand under my feet; I sang because my transformation was complete. I sang the dawnsong—the sacred melody that the men of my people sing, standing on the roof of the men's quarter every morning.

Since then, I had not sung again. As it had for the decades before, the sacred melody sat like a lump in my throat, and I could neither voice it nor swallow it.

I did not know how much time passed, but when I lifted my gaze from the sand where I knelt, I saw Uiziya, the dun-colored carpet still over her shoulder.

Uiziya was a friend from earlier days, when I was young and full of hope still, but now I did not know her that well. She was always at gatherings, weaving with the others—weaving even my own cloth of winds preparing for my transformation, but she did not say much. She was Benesret's niece, and I asked about Benesret, but the others were wary of Uiziya speaking. Every time she opened her mouth to speak of her aunt, she was shushed.

Now she came closer. Her shadow, broad and round, fell over me, sheltering me from the glare of the sky. The carpet she carried over her shoulder stirred, whispering in a language I did not understand.

"Why did you come back here?" she asked.

I looked away. "You would not understand."

Uiziya shrugged. "I think I do. It is not hard to be a changer among my people. I know that it is not true everywhere, but in the great Burri desert, changing your body to match your heart is not a thing to bleed your eyes over."

"It is for me." Of course, she would say this. She grew up here, the vast Burri desert ruled by the Old Royal, who was a changer themself, and welcomed all changers. I was from Iyar.

"I know it is hard for you, heart." Uiziya stretched out a hand, but I made no motion or word to welcome her touch, and she pulled back.

"If I was from the desert," I said, "Benesret would weave my cloth of transformation then and there, when I saw her first when I was twenty-four and she was forty and wise and splendid under the ancient discolored weavings in her tent."

"If you were from the desert," echoed Uiziya, "you would not need Benesret. You would have the cloth woven for you by family, if any were gifted enough. Or you would travel southeast to the Old Royal's capital, and transform at the Sandbird Festival. You would make the transformation as a youth, and go sit with the men and go speak with the men and go guard with the men, and sire children as a man, and raise children as a man, and think no more these noisy, agitated thoughts of yours."

I did not want to think my noisy, agitated thoughts, but they sat better with me than the matter-of-fact, "everything is perfectly commonplace about a swarm of sandbirds cocooning your body and helping you transform, and then you just go sit with the men" conversation I'd had with so many Surun' people. I was not Surun'. I was not from the desert at all. As a Khana person from Iyar, I did not fit, among women, among men. Even far away from home, with only myself for company, I did not fit.

I did not want to wound her, but I did not know how to talk to anyone anymore.

"Forgive me. I think you would understand better if you were a changer."

She lowered herself down slowly, as if the movements pained her, until she sat by my side. "I, too, am a changer."

"Oh?" I frowned, uncomfortable. I had always assumed—I shouldn't have assumed—how could I have assumed? "Forgive me."

Uiziya shrugged. "I made my own cloth of transformation when I was a child."

I did not know that she was a changer, like me. I never thought anyone was. I had never met others who went through the change in Iyar. They were banished or imprisoned or hiding or dead. But here, in the desert, changing one's shape was a matter of ritual, of love, not of desperate secrets.

Uiziya kept speaking. "The first weave is the weave of change, the first mystery of the everchanging desert, the first of the Four Profound Weaves that Aunt Benesret taught me. I wove my cloth of winds, and sandbirds came to me, like they did to you. They cocooned me and burned without burning, and when they were done, I was myself in my body."

"I did not know," I said again. "I'm sorry."

"Nobody remembers anymore. I do not think about it too much. It was a relief. I'd always been a little girl."

We were face to face, Uiziya crouching, me kneeling, and between us the finest threads of sand whispered each to each in a language I did not understand. No longer dun, the carpet of sand undulated with every shade of yellow and brown and gold, and between these strands I saw glimpses of sunset and shadow, and bones—always bones—bones of strange, beguiled animals that had once roamed the desert before the goddess Bird brought our people here, and our stars.

"Why did you return to this place?" Uiziya asked again. She had a habit of asking the same question over and over until she was satisfied.

Because I was running away. No, that wasn't it. "Looking for something."

"Yes?"

My song. I had it for the brief moment after my transformation, but now it felt farther away from me than ever before. *My people.* Except they were far, in Iyar, behind layers of walls, and I did not want to go back.

"My name," I said at last. "I always thought Benesret would give it to me when I came back here, came back to her, ready at last to transform. But when I came back, she was gone."

"They exiled her," said Uiziya.

"Why?" I asked. "Why did they exile her?"

"Because they were afraid."

Uiziya e Lali

The nameless man swallowed. Remembering, no doubt, the first time he came here with his lover

Bashri-nai-Leylit, looking for the greatest carpet ever woven, to bring back to the Collector.

How Benesret greeted them, helped them. How she wove for them.

"Are you afraid of Benesret?" he asked at last.

I shrugged. "I am not afraid of death. I think I will welcome it. I would give my death to her willingly if only she would teach me." Such raw yearning was in my voice that it scalded me, scared me. In response, the nameless man's magical deepnames glittered for a moment in his mind, like warm stars flaring, then settled before I had a chance to see them clearly.

"I do not want you to die," he blurted out, his eyes on the ground.

"You do not want me to die or to sell my carpet," I said, frustration knotted with amusement in my voice. "What would you want me do, nameless man?"

"Nen-sasaïr." The rustle of it was so soft on his lips I almost missed it. "It is just a way-name, until I am given one that is mine."

"Nen-sasaïr," I echoed. "Sandbirds, and . . . ?" I did not know the other word.

"The son of sandbirds. Nen: a son. I would be called my father's son, if I was a Khana man."

"You are a Khana man," I said, but saying this, I knew that I would be rebuked.

"I do not fit anywhere," he said. "Except that I fit with the sandbirds for a brief moment, when I put on the cloth of winds and the sandbirds came to me;

when everything sang and swirled and I sang, too, I sang the dawnsong which had been forbidden to me all my life, a religious rite for the glory of Bird's hidden brother, the singer god, Kimri."

I remembered the melody from his ritual, yes, devastating and joyous, a promise, a cresting of dawn on his lips, in that moment when a dream was becoming, and the fragility of becoming was not yet revealed in nen-sasaïr's heart. "Will you sing the dawnsong again?"

"No. Maybe. I don't know. Sometimes I feel the god—Kimri—just there, behind me, waiting for my song where I cannot see. But I am silent. Khana women are forbidden to sing. I am a man—so I am allowed to sing, but I cannot. My body feels mine like never before; I am whole in my body, but my people will never accept my changing. The thought of it stoppers my throat."

"You should talk to your people," I said. "Talk to them before you decide whether or not they would accept you."

His face flooded with a feeling I could not name. "I can't, Uiziya. And I won't. I want to talk to Benesret."

His hand stirred the dry, hard ground by the carpet of sand, as if he wanted to touch the fringed knots and did not dare. He did not look up when he spoke. "We should find her. Perhaps she will teach you. Perhaps she will give me my name."

I laughed so bitterly the strands of the carpet of sand shook and moved. "If she wanted to teach me, she would return, exiled or no—with all her power of death, with all her knowledge she would teach me. She weaves the white clothes for the Orphan's assassins—do you think mere mortals would stop her? She came to my tent once . . ." I stopped. I did not want him to know my secret.

To master the weave of death you must embrace death. Are you ready?

I thought I was ready then, but I wasn't. Afraid for my children. Myself. Perhaps I was ready now. But nen-sasaïr would reject me like all the others did when I told them. "You will not like me when you learn my secret. You will not want to journey with me."

"Try me," he said, his eyes still firmly on the ground. "If nothing else, I am brave." In his mind, his magic flared again. He did not shroud his mind, so I could see it clearly: three deepnames of different lengths, a single-syllable, a two-syllable, and a three-syllable. A rare and powerful configuration that could not be easily defeated; the Builder's Triangle, as it was called in his land.

My carpet stirred in response to this magic, the eddies and whirls of sand around slivers of bone that transformed for a moment into bejeweled lizards and snakes, then smoothed out again.

I did not want this moment to end.

It would end when he knew me better.

Everything ends. What would happen if he disdained me? I could just sell my carpet as I wanted. "Then I will show you. My secret. And then you'll decide."

"Yes," nen-sasaïr said.

"If you'll watch my carpet, I'll go get provisions. And then we should travel south from here, travel in cool hours and rest when the sun is hottest."

"Yes," nen-sasaïr said again. Not questioning anything.

"How will you travel?" I asked him.

"On sand-skis. I'll show you when you return."

I saw no sand-skis. I wondered if he'd simply take my carpet and leave; but when I made my way back, my breath short from carrying supplies in the heat, my carpet was still there. And nen-sasaïr was still there, his slim, tall frame shifting on two longish, wide planes of bent wood.

In his mind, nen-sasaïr's deepnames flared one by one: first the weakest, the three-syllable, like a thin line of light; then the two-syllable, a short, strong line; and finally, the single-syllable, bright like a star—the strongest of them. His deepnames connected to each other, light running between them until they formed a triangle, then spilled their power onto the sand-skis.

"The blades will float just above ground. It's as if I am gliding on air."

"Me too. On my carpet." I wanted to smile at

him, but I had forgotten how. The motion of my lips stretched my face in odd ways.

The Four Profound Weaves. A carpet of wind, a carpet of sand, a carpet of song, and a carpet of bones. Change, wanderlust, hope, and death.

Nen-sasaïr watched me intently as I breathed my deepnames into the carpet of sand. It floated, lifting me above ground, carrying me out of the encampment, where the tents of my people swayed in the wind, empty. They all were trading, but I had not even tried to sell my carpet, and I did not look back. My weave of wanderlust floated over the boundary spirals drawn in the dust, over the guardian snakes that lifted their heads in recognition and farewell, then settled.

My past lay ahead, and its secrets. The wind and the sand to all sides. Behind me, nen-sasaïr followed.

I had woven the carpets of air and sand. Benesret's great carpet had been made of song. Only death was missing now.

II.
WANDERLUST

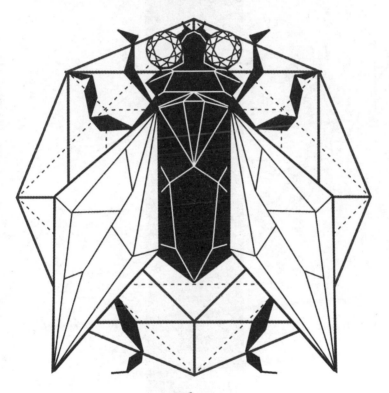

THE
GREAT BURRI
DESERT

nen-sasaïr

We traveled in silence through the cooler hours—I
on my sand-skis, Uiziya floating ahead of me, only
slightly above ground. I had known her for forty
years—no, I had only known her briefly, forty years
ago. When we were both young. When I traveled
with my lover Bashri-nai-Leylit on a desperate trading venture to find the greatest treasure ever woven,
to buy our other lover's life from the Collector.

It was strange to travel with someone again.
Uiziya and I, we were not lovers. Friends, perhaps.
Two people making a journey together. I did not
know where we were going, but I followed Uiziya.
Closer to the encampment, I saw the dun grasses
and shrubs that clung to patches of ground; then,
deeper into that domain, the vegetation became even
scarcer and drier, and the sandhills began to waver
in my sight. I waited for the wind to shift the layers
of sand, revealing to me its secrets like years before,

29

but I saw no miracles this time. Just the sand and the dust in the wake of Uiziya's carpet, the sun—even in cooler hours—forever following me.

I had left my grandchildren behind without even saying goodbye.

Aviya—Aviya-nai-Bashri—my granddaughter was an adult now, and a fine trader, traveling with an oreg of her own. The newly formed Aviya oreg consisted of my granddaughter and her lover, Aviya-nai-Lur—and they would be all right. The two had already made a journey of their own, from Iyar to the desert. And they had taken good care of Kimi.

Kimi, a child of eleven summers, a child we named after the men's god Kimri, a child who was neither a boy nor a girl, who back in Iyar could not be recognized, but here, in the desert, could thrive with an ease that required no discussion. A child who did not talk, a child who wove butterflies from wind, a child whose first-woven carpet was sold to my tormentor.

I did not recall having stopped or closing my eyes, but I must have. I stood there, not willing to look or think of anything, until the rough, grainy threads of a carpet brushed over my face, and I smelled the old threads and dust of Uiziya's carpet. I opened my eyes into sand-cloud in which dim shapes moved and transformed into others, then closed them, my fists in my sand-scrubbed eyes. I coughed and rubbed my eyes and swayed, and Uiziya waited, but not very long.

"What troubles you?" she asked.

That I left my grandchildren to fend for themselves among your people.

I was glad I did not speak this. The Surun' people were our friends, not adversaries. My grandchildren wanted to travel without me, had traveled on their own before. They would continue to be safe. Perhaps. Probably. Likely.

My problem was different.

I said, "All my life, I was a man. And yet I kept that a secret. Not because I wanted to keep such a secret, but because other people told me that I must, that it was shameful and wrong to reveal it, that it was selfish to be who I was. I had to remain—a lover, a trader, a grandmother. I was a reluctant grandmother, but now that I'm free, now that I am a grandfather, am I supposed just not to care for them anymore?"

"Why is there a difference?" Uiziya shrugged. "You can choose to care or not, as all people do."

But in my culture, we never even saw the grandfathers. They were behind the inner white wall. As a part of a traditional family-trading group, called an oreg, a small group of women lovers made trading journeys together, returning to the outer quarter of Iyar. There they met with their husbands only for rituals, in the special rooms tucked in-between the outer and inner parts of the Khana quarter. Grandmothers raised the children while the young women traveled and traded.

And I did not fit. I never fit.

"You make it sound so simple, nen-sasaïr. What your people do, what your people don't do. What they told you to do. What they did not tell you to do, but you think they told you to do. What you think your lovers thought. What you think they think now that they died. Always you lived in the shadow of these people and their rules. Even forty years ago. But nobody's world is clear and simple, much as we want it to be."

"You did not live my life," I said. "And yet you judge me."

She laughed, bitterly. "Judge you? Me? Who am I to judge anyone?"

"You lived your life openly . . ."

She cut me short. "You do not know me. And if you knew, you would surely judge me."

"I wouldn't—"

"No? How can you know?" She seemed angrier now, her carpet swirling with visions of bones and jewels. I took a step back, not from her, from the dust and the threads that once again threatened my face. "I am not afraid."

She looked me up and down. "Then let me show you."

She turned away and I followed. The sand was different here, as if freer, wilder, stirring about the visions of bones and wind. I remembered moments like these from before, when I traveled with Bashri-nai-Leylit, so full of desperate hope for our venture. I was twenty-four then, but now I was sixty-four, and Bashri-nai-Leylit was dead, and Bashri-nai-Divrah was dead, and the world was very short on hope. But even my bones sang the need to wander.

Uiziya e Lali

My carpet shifted as I shifted my weight. It was slightly too large for just one person sitting; another person would balance it out, but I worried my weight made it sag. Benesret had been thin, almost skeletal always, but I was a woman of size. I'd woven this carpet at sixteen. I was big then, too, but I wanted back then to be slim like Benesret, to be lithe and limber like the snakes in our encampment. I wanted to cast a long, elegant shadow. I had always been big, but at sixteen, I had not yet embraced it, so I'd woven my carpet for a thinner person. It carried me well, even now, but it wasn't well-balanced; the tasseled edges rose up as it moved.

"I will teach you to weave from sand," my aunt had said to me back then, *"the second mystery of the ever-changing desert. A weave of wanderlust: the second of the Four Profound Weaves I will teach you until you are ready to put together my loom."*

I had never been ready to put together a loom. The one I continued to use was the training loom that I'd made at sixteen. Others in the encampment gossiped at first, then they stopped, thinking perhaps that I had persisted with such a simple, small frame as a boast about my skills. But my craft, like the frame, had not grown much after I wove this very carpet of sand that carried me now. It whispered of wanderings, and of bones, always bones, for I had woven bones into it—sparsely, as decoration, peeking out of the sand-weaves in glimpses of white. The true weave of bones I had not mastered, for that was the last of the four—the weave of death Aunt Benesret said she would teach me when I was ready. I'd have learned it perhaps, if I hadn't drawn away—from her, from this place.

Oh, this place.

I made my carpet stop. Nen-sasaïr, also deep, perhaps, in his thoughts, kept moving until we were level. We stood side by side on a small outcropping. Below us, we saw collapsed tents, their weavings half-gnawed by time and transformations that happen in the desert when nobody looks. Ghost snakes slithered in the dust, their skeletons glimmering white from their long, limber bodies of smoke.

Nen-sasaïr turned to me. "What is it that I'm seeing, Uiziya? Are these things dangerous?"

"Only if you are afraid to die." I was beyond such things. My life was over.

"What is there?" He was pointing out at a tent that still stood proud. Or so it seemed. It was smaller, white and embroidered blue—but it wasn't embroidery we saw. It was covered in insects. Brilliant, sparkling, winking in and out of sight.

"My husband. This is why we came here. Look."

nen-sasaïr

The brilliant insects shifted about. I saw a young woman, brown-skinned and beautifully large, her face so full of yearning and hope. Uiziya in her youth, as I met her all those years ago, perhaps just a little bit older. She opened the fold of her tent and peeked out tentatively as the stars shone, but these were just pinpricks and slivers of light from the flies.

The flesh-and-blood Uiziya said, "You see other lives as easy because you don't see them. You see your story as complex and hard because you know it best."

"I am sorry," I said. "I didn't mean to imply that you had no hardship."

"I was so full of hope after I saw your great carpet of song being woven. Again and again I pleaded with my aunt to teach me the remaining weave. The weave of death."

"Did she? Benesret?" Out of the corner of my eye, I saw something white flash, a motion, around the tent.

"She said to me, 'Do you know what it means? What it means to weave from the people you care for, from sisters, from lovers, from kin? What it means to weave out of your body, your flesh, to weave your own death as if you saw it for the first time?' Her eyes were hungry but still I said, *teach me. Please, teach me.* So she tried."

"What happened?" I whispered.

"Let us go down."

"Something is there," I said, in a warning, but Uiziya shrugged.

"Something is always there."

We trekked down, until we stood in front of the brilliant buzzing tent. Uiziya drew open the flap, and then suddenly there was movement. Too quick for my eyes to follow at first. A youth, his eyes wide and startled, clutching a handful of white cloth in his right hand. His left held a knife, and he lunged. I breathed, and my names flared to life, but not quickly enough. The youth pushed past Uiziya, the knife making a long, thin graze on her arm as he past her, Uiziya's blood spraying him and the white cloth he held. The youth ran. I formed my Builder's Triangle as fast as I could, but my magic was not that of offense.

Uiziya called after me, "Don't pursue!" as the

youth's lean, wavering shadow ran up and out of the ghost encampment. Out of sight.

Uiziya e Lali

Nen-sasaïr stepped closer to me. He looked shaken. My eyes still trailed the youth, who escaped, and who seemed real enough, just desperate and thin. A fail-out from the Orphan Star's School of Assassins, looking for my aunt's cloth. And weren't we all?

"May I heal you?"

I startled, only now noticing the shallow wound in my arm and the seeping blood that darkened the dun of my dress. It was hard to know what was real, in this place; I felt pain, but as if at a remove, as if nen-sasaïr's voice brought me back to the now in which I could feel pain.

"Yes," I sighed. "Go ahead."

The cut wasn't deep. I watched him carefully apply his magic in a healing weave upon my arm. If recently dealt, flesh wounds could be healed with powerful deepnames quite easily, repaired while the body still remembered itself before the injury. But I was no longer even sure what was real.

"What was that?" nen-sasaïr asked as he tucked the last strands of magic into my flesh.

"An assassin." Far to the southeast, the star of assassins slumbered under the earth, its powerful tendrils spreading the song of strictness and yearning and welcome to all who despaired. To orphans and cast-outs and those disdained by kin. I'd heard that song myself once, long ago. Before I transformed.

"What was an assassin doing here?" nen-sasaïr asked.

"I think he is a fail-out," I said. "If he wanted to kill me, he would have. But no, he was looking for cloth, to prove his worth again to the headmaster. You cannot be an assassin without it, for it is the cloth of death. When death is your pursuit, it protects and conceals you until it is time to strike."

Again, I opened the flap of the tent. Nen-sasaïr shifted nervously, magic at the ready, but there was nobody else inside; nobody alive. There were bones heaped in there, upon carpets that once were bold-colored, and now were bleached almost to whiteness. Upon them were bones gnawed by the insects, and brilliant bones overlaid by more bones. A torn-up piece of white cloth covered them: an offering or a memory.

I said, "My aunt weaves this cloth for those who graduate from the assassins' school. She is paid lavishly, and all this cloth is woven from bones." I thought of this often, how death calls to death, and how she was called to create these clothes for the assassins, for the Orphan Star under the earth. I wanted to learn this craft. I wanted her to teach me.

I wanted so much. But she came to my tent when I was out with the children, and she touched my husband Lali until he lay bloodless on these carpets I'd made.

"What happened?" nen-sasaïr asked.

"She asked, 'Are you ready to weave from death? You must weave from death that matters to you,' but I did not know what she meant. I was confused. So she said, 'I will show you.' So my husband died, and she fed on him, and my people ran. I did not know if I believed them at first. 'Death is the greatest art,' she said, 'the greatest weave of the four. To weave a true weave of death is the greatest calling.'"

My aunt had woven from her husbands, first. Nand had been sick, and I was still unsure if his death had been natural. Divyát . . . nobody suspected at first, not until Lali's death; but then my people began to talk about these and other deaths, and Benesret's name could no longer be spoken among us. I was not sure about anything. Except that she cared for them, except that I still had waited for her. I had seen her weave from hope—from hope!—the greatest hope in the world she had made, and let it go to nen-sasaïr, to help him.

I wanted to understand.

I waited for her to return, to explain. Waited for her to apologize. Waited for her to teach me. For forty years since Lali's death, I waited.

And all my weaves since then had been lifeless,

and people whispered behind my back. I was neither theirs nor Benesret's, nor even mine. I did not want Lali to die. I did not want to learn my craft from his death. But I did not want to stop waiting.

nen-sasaïr

Uiziya's face was turned away from me. "If you changed your mind and do not want to travel with me anymore, I would understand. I won't hold you."

She waited for me to reject her, I saw, or to silence her, just like her kin had done. We both wanted to find Benesret, but now I understood why the others refused to talk of her. Benesret had woven from hope for me, but Benesret was responsible for deaths, and I was not sure what I'd find if I continued.

I could have turned back—turned back where? To the snake-Surun' encampment and my reluctant grandchildren? To Iyar, and all the people in the Khana quarter? Uiziya asked me again and again why I wouldn't talk to my people. But there wasn't *my people* in this, there were women and men—never any in-betweeners that I knew about—just women and men, each on their own side of the wall.

The very thought of coming back to the Khana quarter, to the inner white wall of the men's domain,

made me queasy with trepidation. If I could not enter—if they did not accept me—would that mean
that I was not a man after all? Would I, having the
heart and body of a man, still feel wrong somehow,
not fully whole if the men of my people rejected me?
I was brave, I had always thought, but I did not want
to know the answer. Not yet. Perhaps never.

It was easier to imagine talking to Benesret than
to contemplate this. And I had told Uiziya that I was
brave. "I will travel with you."

Uiziya sighed. "Very well. If you want to find Benesret, we should follow the diamondflies. They feed
on death and feed her, and she feeds on all the death."

We left the ghostly encampment and traveled
south through the desert made once more ordinary.
We rested in the heat, and with darkness we traveled again, following the sparkle of diamondflies and
glimpses of bone revealed and concealed by the wind.

I had never been this far south in the great Burri
desert. At the dawn of our lives, on our first trading
journey, Bashri-nai-Leylit and I had gotten only as
far as the snake-Surun' encampment. We journeyed
in hope and in fear, for the Ruler of Iyar had imprisoned our lover; and he would free her if we brought,
in exchange, the greatest treasure ever woven.

Its threads were spun of song, and it was made
from these threads by Benesret e Nand e Divyát, a
weaver who sat under the faded embroidered awnings in her tent. She wove not from death then, but

from song; and weaving from song was an ancient tradition known to no other kin but the snake-Surun'. Yet among all the other snake-Surun' weavers in their tents, Benesret alone knew the secrets of all the desert's profound weaves. As she had no children of her own, she would bequeath this craft to the child of her closest kin. Uiziya.

Darkness was falling over the dunes, and the cry of the swaddlebird came from the gloom, calling out a warning to its mate. I was once oreg-mate to two of my lovers, but now I was the last of the three to remain.

"Look!" Uiziya's carpet stopped, and she pointed forward. I saw something swirling there, dense darkness in the dusk, like guardian snakes undulating in the evening sand of the Surun' encampment. Feeding.

"What is it?" I asked, swallowing the other question.

"I'm afraid it's somebody we know."

Uiziya e Lali

My carpet floated closer. The darkness tugged and beckoned at me with a secret buzz, and out of it I saw a cloud of diamondflies swarming over a body.

The young assassin. His body under the swarm of

the diamondflies was almost whole, but his arm and hand were missing from the elbow, where my blood had spilled on the white cloth he had taken from the tent. He had touched my aunt's work, and now he was food. My aunt had been banished, because they feared if she stayed, her workmanship would have killed not only Lali, but everybody else as well—goats, children, women, men, in-betweeners, even the snakes that guarded us—everyone.

It has not been a day since we encountered the assassin, but the body I saw now had lost all human integrity under the shreds of its piece of cloth, no longer brilliant white. The smell was horrible, putrid, with a strange green tang, and I pushed my sleeve in front of my nose to shield myself from the worst.

"It is full of stars," said nen-sasaïr, behind me. His voice was tense.

"No, just diamondflies. Feeding." I needed to get away from here. And I needed to stay.

I exhaled, calling on my two deepnames. One-syllable and three-syllable, a configuration which our people called the Weaver's Promise. Nen-sasaïr's magic was more powerful; mine was not known for its strength, but for its uses in craft.

I extended my magic and let the light push past the feeding diamondflies and touch the slip of be-smirched cloth and the body beneath it, now being absorbed into the magic my aunt had made. My touch conjured a brief vision of the person in life.

Yes, it was the assassin we had seen. A young person, their face twisted in so much bewildered anger. Far to the southeast, underneath the School of Assassins, the great Orphan Star slumbers, its power almost as great as that of the two sibling gods. Those who had tasted despair come to it, to train as assassins. I heard they train the anger out of you in that school, or else you fail.

I redirected the flow of my magic and folded my deepnames back into my mind. My touch had been gentle. Some of the diamondflies lifted off and away, but most continued to feed.

"Let's go," I said.

"Why did he die? He did not seem wounded to me, just distraught . . ." Nen-sasaïr had also seen the apparition of the dead youth, and horror tinged his voice.

"I don't know. But we should go see Benesret. It's not far. These flies feed her, see." I wondered if she knew now that we were coming. I should have offered to turn back, but I did not. Nothing waited for me back at home, except the traders and the knowledge that I could not weave or live like before. And all these visions of death disturbed me and drew me forward.

We left the body behind. As soon as it could no longer be seen, nen-sasaïr stopped and bent over. Floating above on my carpet of wanderlust, I watched him retch and heave, and I did not say a thing.

nen-sasaïr

We traveled southeast into the true night. Stars spun and rustled above us like predatory diamondflies, waiting for me to lose my balance and fall. But I would not let it happen. No. I was old, and I wanted to live. This was my true life, life in the new body made by the cloth of winds and by the sandbirds; I could not figure out my place or my name, but this I knew: I wanted to live for decades still, to taste the world in my true body.

"Benesret—" I said, just to break the silence. I did not turn, but I put some power into my words, so that Uiziya would hear. "Benesret—all those years I thought she was exiled because of an affair, or—"

"Because she had two husbands?" Uiziya laughed, but there was no joy in it. "No, it's not a punishable offense, or an offense at all, among our people—"

In the distance I saw a kind of hill, an outcropping of hard rock overgrown—no, studded—with thin dry reeds, which were topped with skulls of jackal and sand-fox and mouse, their eyes glowing with bluish magical lights. Human and animal bones formed the palisade. Behind that grate was a Surun'-style tent—but instead of reed poles, it was supported by curving tusks of the great razu beast, the legendary creature nobody had seen alive in the desert. The pink of the tusks had turned pale green and petrified millennia ago, when nothing else existed. And all the bones glowed in the near-darkness, reflecting starlight and the pallid blue light from the skulls.

The diamondflies had terrified me, but not like this. No. I wanted to live. Not rush headlong into death.

I turned on my sand-skis, but Uiziya lowered the sand-carpet and gripped my sleeve, unbidden. "Please. I want, after all these years, to talk to my aunt. If you leave without me, you will get lost in the sands."

I wanted to protest, before I could open my mouth, she hissed, "If you offend her, maybe the diamondflies will feed on you next."

"Benesret was my friend," I said angrily. "She would not do that to me . . ."

"Then why are you running away?"

"I . . ."

Bluish light poured out of the tent of bones, and stars swirled overhead in rapid motion, revealing a pink glistening in the eastern sky. Night had not yet fully fallen. And yet—

The light within the bone tent grew brighter. A withered, stooped figure emerged and gingerly sat down at the entrance. I heard a voice that chilled and welcomed me.

"My friend, you say. Yes, I remember. I've woven from air a cloth of transformation for you. And also I had woven another, much larger. From song. Oh, that carpet of song. For your master."

"The Ruler of Iyar is not my master," I said.

"Aunt, oh aunt." Uiziya seemed about to burst into tears.

"Hush, child," said Benesret, and I almost smiled to be so called. It meant she was ancient, and we were not so ancient yet. "Hush, child," she said again, and I realized that meant Uiziya, not me. "Come sit at my feet."

Uiziya hurried forward, faster than I had seen her move, then lowered herself on the stone ground by Benesret—the one whose name, for forty years, I had repeated like a promise, like hope. I looked on, at her parched skin, her sunken eyes, and remembered the diamondflies over the old tent. How could Uiziya—

But then Benesret took pity upon me, and this startled me. "I am glad you claimed your true shape, child. Thus one of my lesser weaves yielded its promise."

"Aren't all four weaves equal?" chimed Uiziya. She was a large and poised woman of sixty and more, but now I could see the child in her, the child who yearned to sit at her aunt's feet and learn, a child who was at peace now, in this moment, despite all the visions we saw.

"The weaves might be equal, child," Benesret said, "But we have our affinities. Isn't it strange that among all my weaves, the one that I wove from song was the greatest of them all?" She looked at me. "I hope the carpet of song bought your lover back, Bashri—though I suppose you are no longer called Bashri?"

I swallowed, hard. By Khana custom, all three of us lovers had taken the name Bashri when we formed our oreg. Bashri-nai-Leylit, our leader. Bashri-nai-Divrah. And myself.

I said, "I have no name, and travel as nen-sasaïr."

"I see." said Benesret. "And your lovers?"

"Bashri-nai-Leylit passed away last year. I traveled back to the snake-Surun' encampment, looking for you."

She waited, still.

I forced myself to continue. "Bashri-nai-Divrah . . . the Ruler of Iyar took her life before we returned with your carpet. It had all been all in vain. I am sorry."

"Death is never in vain," said Benesret e Nand e Divyát, "for from it I weave this time and place."

Around us, dawn was crowning the sky with striations of pink and orange. It was no time yet for dawn, but she had made this time with her weaves. Above in the trembling dawn, an ancient, perished razu beast made of bones was laboring to fly.

She could make anything, and what she made and made was bones.

"You sought me out for a reason," she said.

"I wanted to find you," said Uiziya. "I still want to learn."

"And you?"

"I, too, wanted to see you." I could have lied, but I wouldn't. "You told me I could transform my body. You have given me a cloth of winds, to give me hope for forty years when I couldn't use it, could not make this choice. But at last I have transformed, Benesret, and now I came to ask you to name me."

She frowned. "Why not name yourself? Why not take a name of one of your dead, your father, your grandfather perhaps—isn't that your people's tradition?"

I averted my gaze. Mumbled. "I . . . I do not know them. The Khana men all live behind the white inner walls . . . I . . . do not remember ever seeing my own father."

"Seek him out then, now that you have transformed."

Uiziya, sitting still and attentive by Benesret's knee, spoke. "Changing is not done among his people."

Benesret snorted, an odd hollow sound. "That's what *he* says. Changing is always and forever done. Everywhere, it is done; in open, in secret. He has gone through the change and so, I assure you, have others."

To this I made no response. Perhaps other Khana

had changed their body, but I knew of no one who had done so and spoke of it openly, or else I would not feel so alone for so long. If there had been others to talk to, perhaps Bashri-nai-Leylit would not be so worried to have my secret revealed, nor asked me to keep it in the first place.

Receiving no answer from me, Benesret spoke again. "Why seek me, a woman of people not your own? Why ask me to name you away from your own people?"

Uiziya said suddenly, "He was running away from the emissaries of the Ruler of Iyar."

"As were you," I hissed.

Benesret raised an eyebrow. "Why were *you* running?"

"I wanted to sell my carpet, but then, I hoped . . ." Uiziya mumbled. "I hope still to be taught."

I said, "I, too, hoped, for you have given me hope when I had none." I had thought about this for forty years. How Benesret, a stranger from the desert, saw me; how she promised me that one day I would come back to the desert and change my body. She was not welcome among her own people anymore, but she had welcomed me, a changer, when I had no hope.

And I thought, too, over and over, how after Benesret would weave my cloth of transformation, I would ask her to name me. Something that wasn't Bashri.

That was my hope, still.

"You both came here, to me, to seek hope?" Benesret laughed, bitterly. "Let me tell you where it went."

Uiziya e Lali

I was sitting at my aunt's feet, like I'd wanted, oh, I'd wanted for so long, but there was a whirlwind of feeling within me now: fear and yearning and darker things I could not look at, much less name. Still sitting, I half-turned, trying to see both my aunt and nen-sasaïr. I was not agile enough for these motions. My body protested as I twisted and turned to try to see both.

My aunt's body shifted as well. She was so thin now, insubstantial almost, in contrast to my own robust size; when she moved, I could almost hear her bones moving of their own accord, like the skeletal razu, a mythical beast she had resurrected, preparing to fly.

"There was a weaver," my aunt said.

Nen-sasaïr had taken off his sand-skis. His face, still and serious, appeared carved of a warm stone. He clasped his hands behind his back, preparing to listen.

"There was a weaver, see, a weaver wise with age but not yet burdened by it, a weaver who had been taught by her grandmother to make, in the ancient Surun' tradition, a cloth out of wind to assist those who sought to change their body in accordance with their innermost heart. The weaver's grandmother had been a changer, but the girl herself was not, and yet joyously did she learn the weave. From near and far, people young and old would come to her—those who could not make the journey to our far-off capital to seek the Old Royal's own assistance—and so they came to her, and she wove for them the cloth of transformation that calls the sandbirds down from the sun."

I could just about see Benesret as that girl. I had been such a girl, plump and studious under the awning of her tent, so full of hope after my wanderings. The first cloth of winds I made was my own. It was so long ago that I had all but forgotten the time before, pushed it out of my mind like a summoning I no longer wanted to hear.

"Weave after weave the girl matured into a young woman, sure of her craft, and yet she still used her grandmother's loom. 'It is time for you to go into the desert,' the girl's grandmother said, 'and learn to weave from sand,' and so I did. I wove of sand, and stepped upon the carpet I made, and gave myself to wanderlust. I traveled south to the heart of the desert, under the whirligig of stars spinning in the darkness above. I stopped at last, and disembarked among the remains of a stone labyrinth. It was a different time, this time I found, ever-changing, always moving, the secret depths of the desert revealed to me by the wind, for I have woven that wind."

It had been nothing like that for me. I simply went out to the regular desert, at sunset, when orange and blue mixed and mingled; I wove of ordinary sand, took a short fly-about on my carpet of wanderlust, and then put it away where it lay unused for those forty years.

Benesret continued her tale. "I opened my arms to the spinning ancient sky and turned, around and around, the sleeves of my garment filling with wind. Everywhere I looked, I saw bones—bones of beasts, forgotten and ancient, dreaming themselves up into visions I had never seen—a bird with two heads, drumming on four bone drums, a stick in each beak and claw; a lizard, illustrious, bejeweled; the great razu beast in flight, its wings unfolding over a desert like a rainbow."

Nen-sasaïr said, "These are the images you wove into the great carpet made of song."

My aunt ignored him. "I knew right then that I was destined to be a great weaver. I would make the Four Profound Weaves and then bring them together, to reveal the greatest secret of all; that the Four Profound Weaves would bring the gods themselves at my bidding, for the desert had revealed itself to me. And everything in it was made of death."

nen-sasaïr

"Bird is the goddess of death." I was not sure why Benesret's tale rattled me so, but I needed to breathe.

"No," said Benesret. At her knee, Uiziya shifted uncomfortably.

"Bird takes us up when we die," I insisted.

"No," Benesret said again.

"It is true. I've seen it happen. She came for Bashri as a dove." I'd lied to my grandchildren when they asked if I had seen the goddess when Bashri-nai-Leylit died. My three deepnames gave me power; and of all of my family, I alone could see Bird, but I lied, said I wasn't strong enough to see what shape the goddess took when the she came for my lover's soul. How could have Bashri-nai-Leylit gotten such a peaceful vision of Bird when all our lives, all my life she had restrained me? She'd pleaded with me and shamed me with my truth of being a man, until the very end.

I did not realize I had spoken these words, but Benesret said, "Did it feel good to conceal the shape Bird took for her?"

"Yes," I hissed, the confession spilling from me unrestrained. "Yes. A dove. Such a small thing to conceal compared to my life of forced secrets, forty years of her refusing me when she knew—" I exhaled. "Yet

I loved her, Benesret, I loved her, and Bird help me, I still do."

"I remember that," she said. "And I see that."

We stood in silence. Rather, she sat, supported by the sitting Uiziya, and I stood like a supplicant in front of them. Pain wrapped around me like a veil, lending all shapes a pallid hue—or perhaps it was the dawn, called unbidden before the night was done, unfolding now over the two Surun' women and their throne of bones. I had been glad to find Benesret alive after all those years, but now I was dizzy and wary. Benesret spoke of the great secret of the weaves, but her hand moved upon Uiziya's shoulder, and a shimmer like diamondflies ran down her long, gnarled fingers.

My lips moved. *Uiziya—*

She nodded at me. *Nothing's amiss.*

Benesret's mouth pulled wide, as if she was smiling, but I was not sure of that either.

"Bird is not the master of death. I steered my carpet of wanderlust south and east over the ever-changing sands, looking for her, but I could not find her. I went to the School of Assassins next, the school built over the buried Orphan Star. The goddess Bird does not come for the assassins, or for their victims. But I learned from the headmaster that they, too, need cloth."

I shuffled on my feet. "You said you would tell me of hope."

"Yes, child." Benesret sighed. "I said no to the headmaster that first time, for I would not weave from death before I wove from song. Tell us why, Uiziya."

"This tale must be told four times," said Uiziya, as if reciting a lesson. "Stitched with wind, stitched with sand, stitched with song, stitched with bones. Change, wanderlust, hope, and death. Only then will the ultimate secret will become known. It is the secret of the sibling gods—the glorious Bird and her hidden brother, the singer Kimri."

"Death," echoed Benesret. "Yes, death, but not yet. First I became *normal*, for that is the word people say. I hid the desert's visions in my heart and went back home to my tent, my two husbands, my goats—I taught my niece and made lesser weaves and I waited. I needed to weave from hope, but I could not envision a hope that would not lead me back to death, to the last of the Four Profound Weaves which I desired so much, but that was not enough.

"One day I took up my carpet of wanderlust and traveled east, calling out for hope to find me so I could be done with my task. I saw a woman of the Maiva'at standing on the edge of her encampment. Her mouth overflowed with melodies that hung in threads down her body. She told me, haltingly, that Bird came to her when she sang, and by singing, she spun these threads out of Bird's own feathers."

"Zurya," I said, for I knew this tale of old, or at least a version of it.

"Yes, Zurya," said Benesret. "I begged her for these threads, so I could weave from them. Such a cloth I would make—I could already see it in my mind, how it would sing with all the colors of Bird's triumphant plumage when she flies over the desert at dawn. But Zurya refused to give me anything, and her eyes were dull with hunger for the goddess. 'I will sing these threads until I can sing no more, because she comes to me, and I spin from her, and I will possess these threads alone.'"

"She wanted to be freed," I whispered. But perhaps that came later.

"Two years later, you showed up—you and Bashri-nai-Leylit—with these threads for trade. I took them up without asking what happened. I could see it myself: Bird forsook her."

I shuddered. "We had found her when she could neither speak nor sing, for the threads had cocooned her completely. We pulled these threads, so she could sing again, but she told me she would not." That had seemed so extraordinary to me then—as Khana women are forbidden from song—that Zurya would refuse to sing ever again, even though she was permitted to do so by her people, even though she could sing so beautifully that she brought down the goddess and spun from her feathers.

Benesret chuckled. "Of course she would not sing again. What hope she had was made into thread, and it choked her. She gave up hope so she would live."

I shuddered again. "Among the Khana, only men are allowed to sing, and Bashri . . ." I stopped to gulp a breath, then continued. "Bashri-nai-Leylit had asked me not to sing."

But she'd also asked me not to walk around the women's side of the quarter in men's clothing, and she'd asked me not to take up underground artifice, for holy artifice was the domain of men; but I did all these other things except sing. I was not sure now why that prohibition had felt holy to me, untouchable. As if my offered voice would offend not just my lover, but the singer-god, Kimri. "I begged Zurya to sing. To sing because I couldn't."

"Did she?" asked Benesret.

"No. What kind of hope is that?"

"I welcomed it," said Benesret. "I took up the threads, and upon my grandmother's loom I made the greatest treasure ever woven, all the hope and brightness of the world, and the images of my visions from the desert: the drumming eagle, the lizard, the razu beast; and then I gave hope away. I gave this treasure to you, for your master."

I said again, wary, "The Ruler of Iyar is not my master."

"He locked all this hope away in his coffers. And now I was free to weave from death."

"And did you?" Uiziya asked, her voice trembling. "Did you bring the weaves together, bring the sibling gods to you?"

She shook her head. "I weave from death for the headmaster of the assassins' school," said Benesret. "It's lesser work. Clothes. But never again from hope. My greatest work is gone, and so I cannot bring the weaves together, and I have no hope left to weave another. And now you know where my hope went."

"I'll go then," I said, uneasy. "To look for it, then."

"Look among your own," Benesret said. "Your Khana people, the men, in their white inner quarter. That's where you always wanted to be."

Perhaps she was right. That I had to overcome my fear of my own people, and go. Perhaps I would find hope then, feel what Zurya had felt so strongly she chose to hoard it, feel what Benesret had sought so desperately only to give it away. For I felt no hope and I needed it, in this place, in all places.

Dawn was past us now, and the rays of the sun licked my face with the promise of oppressive brightness to come, bringing with it an intent that kindled inside me like dry reeds.

"Go with him, then," said Benesret to Uiziya.

"But Aunt—I want to stay with you and learn—"

"Yes?" Diamondflies rose off Benesret's body, and settled upon Uiziya. "Do you understand what awaits you here, child?"

"Yes," Uiziya said. "Yes, I am ready."

"You refused to learn from Lali's death; is that why you brought him . . ." she nodded at me, ". . . as a price of your learning?"

I recoiled, understanding it all in a bright moment. Uiziya's friendship, her desire to travel with me—all was a ruse, to lure me, to bring me where I could become the sacrifice, the significant death she would weave from. I inhaled sharply, but before I could do anything, Uiziya spoke.

"Not him," she said. "Myself."

My cheeks flooded with blood, and I swallowed my shame. I'd assumed the worst of Uiziya, the deepest betrayal, when at every step she'd asked if I wanted to continue, taken me to her aunt when I asked and she wasn't yet sure she wanted to go.

"Yourself?" Benesret said.

"Yes, Aunt."

"Do not tell me this, child," Benesret said. The diamondflies moved down, wrapped Uiziya's right leg with brightness. "For you know what I need is sustenance."

"Uiziya, no!" But I was not fast enough, and still I did not fully understand.

"Take what you need from me," Uiziya cried, and the diamondflies dug into her flesh, gorged themselves.

I took a step forward. I thought she'd betray me. Give me to be consumed like Lali in his tent. But she hadn't. And I would not let her be taken.

I locked my gaze with Benesret. "Stop it. Stop."

"Or else?" She stared right back at me, but her eyes were unfocused. Drawing in power, drinking in my friend's life in all its brightness. "She came to me. She asked. She consented."

I pulled on my powerful deepnames, forming of them a triangle. Benesret laughed, and I could have laughed with her if I wasn't so angry and so terrified, for there was no way I'd defeat such a person. Behind Benesret, the razu beast reared, its eyes ruby red; and flanking her, I saw ghost assassins in their white, unsullied robes. Even the youth from before was there, the one her diamondflies had consumed; one of his eyes was a maze that led into the Orphan Star's depths.

Still I stepped forward. Benesret was feeding. Not as powerful.

"You wish me to take you, too? Like she wished to be taken?"

It was useless to fight with Benesret. I had to use my trading skills, my promising skills, like I once used with the Collector, bargaining for my lover's life.

"I'll bring you back the carpet of song that you made in the dawn of our lives, the greatest carpet ever woven, the third of the Four Profound Weaves."

"What do I need it for?"

"It is hope."

"Hope is with the Ruler of Iyar, the Collector," she said. "Guarded, I assure you, by the finest of assassins all wearing the cloths I have woven. Hope has been locked away, child."

But I saw that she was interested.

"I will find it and bring it back to you, and you'll put it together with your other weaves. Call the sibling gods closer."

"Ha! Forever you ferry that thing back and forth. It is dangerous to have so much hope. Even the Collector knows it, which is why he has locked it away." But her stream of diamondlflies weakened.

"I will find it and bring it to you," I snarled through my teeth. "I've done it before. I will do it again. Let her go. Let her go. *Let her go.*"

The diamondflies rose off Uiziya's body. She toppled forward, face into the dirt, and I caught her. She was breathing. Unconscious.

Benesret reabsorbed the diamondflies into her body, looking, for a brief moment, content; yet still hungry. "Then take her and go."

Quick. Quick. I had to heal her, but it was too dangerous here. I shifted Uiziya's body onto her carpet of sand. Her leg bled and convulsed under the now-tattered dun dress. I stepped onto the carpet next to her, abandoning my sand-skis. I pulled on my deepnames, trying to make Uiziya's carpet float. She had a different deepname configuration than mine, a weaker, subtler one, and the carpet was attuned to her. And it was thin. We were too heavy, together, on this carpet. I was not sure that I could make it work.

My eyes were still locked on Benesret's. I should not have trusted her, should not have sought her, should not have been lulled by her tale. Yet she had stopped, for now. In the blossoming daylight, the bones of Benesret's tent glowed pink and triumphant with Uiziya's stolen blood.

Benesret spoke. "Yes, my carpet of song is missing from me to complete the great pattern. But I would never be content for my greatest work to be that of hope. I'll feed on all I've ever loved and weave the desert's greatest carpet out of bones. I have been studying death all my life, waiting for that. Yet I'm letting her go, as I let the carpet of song go with you forty years ago. Don't betray me again. Bring it back. Bring her back."

I could not make sense of her words, of the world. She could have killed us both easily, I knew now, killed us before we even saw her.

She said, "Take care of each other."

I made the carpet float at last, and steered it west, toward Iyar.

III.
HOPE

THE
SPRINGFLOWER
CITY OF IYAR

nen-sasaïr

I left Iyar as if a lifetime ago, but it had only been months. I left on my sand-skis and veiled like a Khana man, in defiance of everyone—Iyari and Khana, strangers and family, and especially in defiance of Bashri, my Bashri-nai-Leylit, whose soul had been carried aloft by a dove. I had sped through the Desert Gate, tossing a scant bribe to the guards, trusting that I would never come back.

Well, I was back.

I remembered my journey west through the desert to the city. The flying carpet, and Uiziya motionless in my arms. The sun forever bearing down, for I did not stop in the heat. The blinding-bright weight of the sky, like the cocoon of sandbirds at my transformation, except that it burned without shielding me, except that there was no joy in it.

Uiziya had not spoken nor awakened. I kept trying to heal her, weaving my deepnames into familiar healing patterns, but even though her injury was fresh, my magic was powerless to undo it. Uiziya's leg felt withered to the touch. Just short of the city's Desert Gate, I shaved my face and retied my sash in a Surun' man style, deciding that it was safer for me to present as a desert man, not Khana. I drew on my deepnames to help me carry her, for fear that a flying carpet would be taken away.

And so I stood at last before the Desert Gate of Iyar. Chiseled stone and roses everywhere, masking the rot underneath. From afar, the briny smells of the sea.

The guards at the gate spoke in the desert's common language, and I was satisfied that they thought me a Surun' nomad. Thank Bird for that, for my people were not allowed to wander the streets of Iyar without a special permit.

"Your sister is diseased," they said. "You cannot bring her in."

"No, no. It's just her leg. I was told I can find a good physicker here." I wanted to make a moving chair for her in the city. This idea had possessed me in the desert as I labored to steer the burdened carpet west. I would make for Uiziya a moving chair, like I'd made once for Bashri-nai-Leylit. This was important to me.

The guards eyed us both warily, but I had plenty of gold from my years of trading, and that helped. Once in the city and out of their sight, I wrapped the unconscious Uiziya in her carpet, and after many attempts, I made the bundle float just slightly, and the burden of Uiziya's body lessened in my arms. I would not be able to carry her long, otherwise.

Now I hesitated whether to put up my veil. Khana people wore veils whenever they ventured out of the quarter, but the men rarely did so, unless they decided to flee the inner quarter forever. And I was supposed to be Surun', Uiziya's brother; that was what I told the guards.

She had a beautiful, ample shape where Benesret's feeding fire had not touched her. The carpet eased the burden; I could not help but notice how all of her now was inert in my arms, given in to a place beyond pain.

I wore no veil as I carried her through the side alleys, out of curious eyes.

Uiziya e Lali

I came to. Didn't it always begin like this? A story, floating somewhere here in the darkness, pulsing with the insistence of pain.

I could not yet open my eyes, but I saw it. Yes. A story without a name. My left thigh, pulsing in the darkness as I pulsed, screamless, though my throat felt scorched and lacerated with screaming, as if I had given birth.

This had been no birth.

Or had it been?

Benesret.

"Take what you need from me . . ." I had said, *take it, take it,* and she took and took. I had asked her to teach me.

The hollowness in my ribcage was greater than pain.

I tried to move. Disoriented.

The hollowness in my ribcage was the Orphan Star, the star of all those rejected by Bird, the star that watches and waits in the earth beneath the School of Assassins. It was darkness buzzing with death, a star made of diamondfly deepnames that fed on its own and could never be satisfied.

The desert had revealed itself to me. And everything in it was made of death.

If I could move my fingers, I could weave from it.

The realization, jolting-yellow with sun's brightness. My eyes peeled open and nen-sasaïr's face swam too close, frowning. "Uiziya? Heart?"

He'd never before called me "heart". When I had called him so, he'd winced.

I tried to speak, but could not. This had been real—bones, and my aunt's hunger, my learning, the pain. Nen-sasaïr gave me water from his flask, and fussed over me until I could open my eyes and see what seemed much less real.

I was not in the desert. A city. Stone walls, and the intensity of verdant smells in the air.

"Iyar," said nen-sasaïr. He looked as if he wanted to speak on, but I could not listen.

I was on a carpet. My carpet of sand. It rested not on sand but on stones that dug into my thighs—my right thigh, where I had sensation. In my left, I did not. I was covered with cloth, stained and bloody, but even though I could not see under it, the shape of my body seemed different at the thigh—no longer wide and plentiful as the rest of me, but charred, immovable. Wilted. That, too, was me, as was my aunt's art and her dereliction.

"It's not as bad as it could be," said nen-sasaïr defensively. "I begged her to stop, and at last she did. It would have been worse if she hadn't."

"All my life I waited," I said. The first words out of my mouth, but I had to force them out somehow. "Waited for her to come back and teach me." She hadn't. She had fed on me instead, just like she had devoured my husband Lali.

I'd asked her for it.

"I tried to heal you," said nen-sasaïr, "but I couldn't. I will get you a physicker. Just a moment of rest now."

I had asked Benesret to take what she wanted because I wanted—I yearned and yearned so much for her touch. And for death? I must have, for all Benesret made and made was death.

That had been a different me. I could no longer remember. I wanted to be her food. I wanted to prove myself to her. That emotion still stirred me.

"What you need . . . what I need to make for you," said nen-sasaïr, "is a moving chair like I made for Bashri-nai-Leylit when she could no longer walk. You could steer it with your deepnames."

He wanted to solve my pain, I saw. To solve and make it better. But I had no thoughts like this. I wanted the pain to stop and I wanted, I wanted to understand who I was now. Where I was. I did not want a moving chair.

"I have my carpet," I said. I had made it myself, before I truly needed it to help me move. I tried to stir now, to change my position, but even a small motion sent sharp waves of pain up my torso, radiating into my chest and throat. I could not breathe properly.

And everything in it was made of death.

Fear flogged me as I gulped the air, stale and perfumed with rot and blooming roses, so different from the expansive desert air. This was Iyar. Iyar. I felt nen-sasaïr's touch on my good thigh. "I need to get you to a place where you can rest."

I turned my head slowly. Tall walls. There was a child here, a child of about eight, and gaunt-looking, with a curious glint of their eye. The child looked at me with that singular hunger that reminded me of Benesret, and I wondered if they were there to witness my death.

I remembered wanting to die before I tasted death. Before I gave myself to Benesret to feed upon, like she fed upon Lali, like she fed and she spun and she fed. I did not want to be food. I wanted to be a weaver. That was what it all was about, that I wanted to be like my aunt. To weave from hope first, like she did before she could learn to weave death.

I tried to speak again. *We need to make it to the palace, to the coffers, to that place where song and hope lay hidden, so I can bring it back to Benesret like she wanted, so I can prove myself to her, so that I would no longer be food, so that I too would weave from death.*

But only gurgling came from my mouth, and after it, the soft yarn of darkness.

nen-sasaïr

"I know a person like this," said the child. I had not noticed when he appeared by my side. I was not even sure if the child was a boy; my time among my Surun' friends taught me that it did not matter. Perhaps this child was an in-betweener, like Kimi.

I wondered if they were a deepname-orphan, one of these children whose mothers could not take care of them after their deepnames were stripped off by force. In the city, giving up one's magic was a rite of passage for those non-Khana women who possessed it, much celebrated as an act of distinction.

Most women continued their lives after such an event, but some of them, once bereft of their deep-name or deepnames, went flat and indifferent. Most got better, but some never recovered. Their children ran wild and barefoot through the city; the mothers could find no solace or reason to continue, the loss of magic more bitter than the veils of death.

And everything in it was made from death.

I left the city seeking change, but now that I found it, it wasn't death but hope that I sought. I had to find a physicker for Uiziya. For her sake, too, I had promised to seek yet again the carpet of hope I had given away forty years ago, attempting to pay for another life.

"*I will weave for you from song,*" Benesret told me once, forty years ago. "*The third mystery of the ever-changing desert: to weave from the colors of rainbow where no rain has fallen on these desiccated sands; for this thread had been spun out of Bird's own feathers, and so I will weave from it, weave in all the desolate places where only silence and despair had been. And look, this weave is hope: the third of the Four Profound Weaves and the greatest treasure ever woven. I will give it to you so that you can trade the Collector for your lover, for Bashri-nai-Divrah, for her life.*"

But Bashri-nai-Divrah was already dead. The Ruler of Iyar had killed her, just like Benesret had already killed Uiziya. It was hopeless. But I did not know what else I could do.

"If you give me a coin, I will tell you."

The orphan was still there, and their words brought me out of my reverie.

"Tell me what?" In the desert a child like this could be called by the headmaster's music to journey southeast and join the School of Assassins. But this child did not seem to have that tell-tale look of blankness. "What would you tell me?"

"What happened to her."

"I know what happened to her." But something stirred in me, and I dipped my hand into the pocket for a coin.

The child took it and tested it against their tongue. A coin of silver, a thin coin from the Surun' encampment, with its three stamped serpents and smoothed ridges. The child's face was curious as they tasted the silver, and licked the heads of the snakes. Satisfied, the child hid the coin in their shirt.

"He brought the rod. And it sucked all the life from Juma, so he was withered. Withered all over, not just one limb, like hers."

I tried to understand, but this tale did not seem to have a beginning. "What are you talking about?"

"When Juma's father came. A month or so ago, now. He was all bent and sad. And he was clean and well-dressed and he smelled of roses, and he said, I do it because I love you."

"I do not understand," I said.

"And all the faces in the rod were leering. His

father touched him with the rod, and Juma fell to the ground. I looked at the rod and saw his face there, too. A small one. His mouth opened and closed, but no sound came." The child took a step away from me. "Is this what happened to your sister?"

"No." But wave after wave of coldness ran down my back. "What happened then?"

"The others ran away. But I didn't. I was afraid, but I wanted to know what happened to Juma. I shook and shook him, but he was already in the rod. I thought his father would kill me. But he just looked sad."

I had paid for the child to speak, but their words made no sense to me. "Do you know who can heal this wound? She is not in a rod. There was no rod. She is still alive."

The child circled closer again. "Maybe. Maybe she is too big to go into the rod." But their face was dubious. "Maybe only her leg went."

"That's not what happened." I felt angry for Uiziya's body to be judged, but I also felt at a loss. "Do you know who can heal this?"

"I heard that a physicker comes to the inn at Three Roses. Ask for the special one, from the palace. But you have to have coin."

I gave the child another coin. They wanted to show me the way to Three Roses, but I refused. Alone with Uiziya's body, I tried to push the strange conversation out of my head.

I had always walked veiled on the streets of Iyar, for our women with magical power were not permitted outside of the Khana quarter unless they were properly veiled. Only Khana women and foreign ones would be permitted deepnames at all; it was illegal for Iyari women to do so, and those who resisted were rebels. As a man or a woman of the Khana, I should be veiled in these streets. My naked face bothered me, the feel of that city air and people's furtive glances made me feel exposed. Then I began to notice how people gave way to me.

Was it because I was Khana, and without a veil? But they likely thought me a person from the desert. I wore Surun' clothing and had called myself Surun' at the gate. Then why did they give me way? I wondered next if it was out of respect for my burden, but some even bowed.

I asked an Iyari woman for directions, surprised by how my own words sounded. Among the Surun' and with Benesret I did not pay much attention to how the changes in my voice affected others. It was just another aspect of my transformation; my friends and even my grandchildren did not remark upon it. Here, in Iyar, my voice rang hoarse and hollow. The woman gave me directions bashfully, lowering her eyes from my gaze, even though I was old.

Yes, this was the reason. That I was a man, and three-named strong. In Iyar, where women were not allowed deepnames and were taught to always speak softly, it mattered.

At the hostel, a lie and a bribe took care of us once again. Uiziya was my sister, as I said at the gate, in need of a physicker. We were both snake-Surun', trader and weaver, hoping for a miracle of healing.

The room we got was of stone, rough-hewn and laid thickly with carpets. They were of poor quality, loosely woven, garish with green and chapa-diluted madder, which made the color look more pink than red. The designs of the carpets were rough, too—diamonds and circles piled on without rhythm or meaning. If I were still trading, I would refuse this offering. I could have afforded better rooms, but this got us closer to the Rainbow-Tiered Court of the Ruler of Iyar.

I made Uiziya comfortable on a low bed piled with these badly made weaves. I paced until my legs ached so much that I could pace no more. I ordered food without either meat or fish; a desert custom, I said. I'd made it up on the spot. My people would eat fish but not meat; if I asked for fish, it could reveal me as Khana, and my people were not welcome in Iyar outside of our quarter, unless in possession of papers. I had never before concealed being Khana.

Secrets. Always secrets. I was weary of secrets,

and wanted to go home, wherever it was. Perhaps I just needed to be alone.

A physicker came, and I paid him, but he told me nothing I had not already known. Uiziya did not wake, and I felt rotten to have shown the physicker her body, for he had shuddered at the sight of Uiziya's leg, but gave us no aid. What healing did I seek anyway? What repair could be had for a wound that was woven from death?

Why had I come here? For hope, but I did not know what hope meant anymore. A carpet. A life. Whose life? Mine, or Uiziya's? I no longer knew. But I was stubborn, and did not want to give up.

I put a sash around my waist and went down to the court once again. I asked if they knew someone else. A better physicker, someone who knew wasting illnesses and would not shy away from uneasy visions of illness.

A special physicker. The one who comes from the palace.

"I have coin," I said, and bribed them even more lavishly this time, weaving my deepnames into the silver to sweeten the offering.

Back in the room, I paced among stifling, thick-woven carpets. Uiziya was not dead. She wasn't withered dry, or gone into some rod. She had woken briefly before, and would wake again. She had to.

The second physicker came. A shorter one, bald and more lavishly dressed, his eyelids painted in green. He brought potions and ointments, and an odd, swinging speculum on a long chain, and he took his time examining Uiziya's leg. But I saw his eye wander and rest upon the carpet of sand, rolled and tucked into a corner.

"What are you looking at?" I asked.

The physicker spoke evasively. "There's many a treasure in the Collector's Rainbow-Tiered Court. Treasures smelted and strung, treasures hammered and burnished, treasures wrought and treasures woven. But among the treasures at the palace, none are greater than the treasures hidden."

"It's just an old rug. My sister used to be a weaver in her youth." I shrugged, pretending indifference I almost but didn't quite feel. "But if you heal her, if she wakes up and speaks, then I have coin and will pay you lavishly."

The physicker nodded, his gaze sliding off mine. "I can give her this for easy sleep." He showed me a deep green vial. "In the morning I'll come again. I'll prepare special potions to help her regain both consciousness and vitality. Does this seem amenable to you?"

"Will she walk again, physicker?"

"Your sister has sustained a grave wound," the physicker said. "How did she come by it?"

"Her aunt."

He frowned. "She might relearn to walk. And the goddess Bird might come to her with new flesh in her beak, as a gift. But you should not hope for it."

"You are harsh," I said. "Unnecessarily. This isn't a jesting matter"

"I do not deal in false promises."

It made me trust him, somehow, that he told me to hope for her life, not her wholeness. "You will come at dawn?"

"Yes," he said. "After the last move of the dawn-song is sung from the roofs of the Khana quarter."

"Then I'll wait for you."

"Yes," said the physicker. "Do."

Night had fallen in the springflower city of Iyar. I paced in the room, denying my body its pain. Uiziya slept quieter now, her breath more even and eased after taking the physicker's potion. I should sleep, too, but I couldn't. I had to go somewhere. Do something.

Do a particular thing, and the need for it gripped me like my hands had once gripped Bashri-nai-Le-ylit's moving chair, after she could no longer steer it with her deepnames. The knuckles of my hands flexed and tightened in memory. I had made the moving chair for her. And now I wanted to make another.

Bashri-nai-Leylit. My lover. My leader. My best friend. My captor. She held such power over me. I let her because I loved her. *Why didn't you leave?* my

Surun' friends asked me. You could have just left. You and all these women who tired of your way of life Yes, I could, and they could. Some women left for trading journeys and never returned, leaving their children behind to be brought up by grandmothers. But most did return. Our people's women were held together by strong webs of love and kinship. Of oreg-mates, lovers. Of sisters and friends. Of grandmothers and their lovers. Of children and their lovers. Those who loved you held you in shape, even if this shape was all wrong.

My lover, my Bashri-nai-Leylit, she did not want me to be a man. If I became a man, then she could not love me, she said. And I loved her. Benesret had woven a cloth of winds for me, a promise that I could come back and transform my body at any time, but Bashri had begged me to stay by her side. I gave her the cloth of winds in the end. For safekeeping. *Give it to me when you're ready*, I said, but she never did.

Still, I had made the moving chair for her when she ailed, and steered it for her after she no longer could move. She was dead now, but my hands still remembered the feeling of the cool white metal I gripped as I walked behind her.

Uiziya was not Bashri. She wasn't my lover. But I was responsible for this wound. If I hadn't asked Uiziya to come with me, she wouldn't have been injured. And I thought—I thought she betrayed me, when she never did.

I got up at least, and called on my three powerful deepnames. Uiziya slept soundly. I warded the door with my magic, then took what I needed and stepped out. There was time yet, before the dawn.

The streets of Iyar were even more fragrant at night, adorned with primrose blooming on balconies and in the tiny gardens; I saw the small purple flowers they called gugrai opening on the parasite vines that cloaked the walls. I wanted to put on a veil, but couldn't find it.

I edged closer and closer to the Khana quarter, my hands gripping at air.

It felt strange to be back. The great double doors of the quarter were open as always at this time of night. It was shameful for Iyari to trade with the Khana people in daylight, so they sneaked in under the piercing regard of the stars. I walked under the outer gray walls, my hands surreptitiously touching the boulders of the quarter, shaped and chiseled before my great-great-great-grandmothers' time. If I squinted hard, I could sense old magic buried in the stone, deepnames planted here centuries ago.

Two Raw Guards flanked the open gate. These were automata created by Khana men for the protection of our quarter from the aggression of outsiders. The Raw Guards were gigantic, fashioned of white enameled metal, unmoving except for their emerald and lacquer eyes, which followed each guest as they entered the gates. Occasionally a Raw Guard's white surface would ripple with the dark wriggles of holy Birdseed writ, and then the automaton would bend and push a person away, gently unless they resisted.

I leaned on a nearby wall and watched the Raw Guards from the shadows for a while. The Khana men made these Guards, made them beyond the white walls of the inner quarter. The Khana scholars. When I was young, I dreamed of making such automata, pinnacles of craftsmanship and faith, but all I had was a secret workshop underground where women labored, making small objects too mundane and unimportant for the labor of men. My greatest work there had been a moving chair for Bashri-nai-Leylit, a work of nothing much in comparison to the Raw Guards.

It was nothing much, but for decades, this work defined me. The underground artifice, and wearing men's clothes, and the companionship of my mentor and my friends who were into such ways, and the scandalous gossip of others.

I missed the work.

I did not miss the others judging me. How they'd say, *It's just the old . . .* I could not even bear to pronounce my old name in my head. *Just the old—Just Bashri-nai-Leylit's old lover running around the quarter in men's clothing!* I was not ready for that regard, not then, not again, now that my truth has been made manifest in my body. I wished I had grown out my beard like the men of my people, not shaved it in Surun' style, but it was too late to undo that.

Finally, I pushed myself off the wall, trying not to dwell too much on my fear. I wore Surun' clothes—would that be enough to conceal me? They knew me. At least, they thought they did. My searching hands grasped a thin piece of fabric in the folds of my garment. The veil had been with me all along.

With trembling hands, I unwound the transparent cloth and tied it around my head to obscure my features. How would this help, I was not sure, but I could not bear the thought of their glances upon me.

I wanted to run away. This was scarier than Benesret's tent of bones. The urge to run was overwhelming, but I needed to help Uiziya. She said she did not need my help, but I had to do something. The chair.

My feet carried me past the unmoving Raw Guards, and into the riot of noise and light.

Here, Iyari and foreign buyers mingled with each other. Khana women young and old ran around, adding magical candlebulbs to wires strung in a makeshift ceiling over the square, which already trembled with hundreds of these colorful lights. Beneath this riot, embroidered and faded shawls were stretched taut between four poles of the booths, each containing Khana women and their wares—jewelry and glass, clothing and carved razu ivory from the desert, spices from all the edges of the land where the Khana traders were permitted to go. The air was perfumed with turmeric and clove, bahra spice and persimmon wine. I breathed easier here, mesmerized by familiar sights and smells, and at once a stranger to them like never before.

"Brother!" someone said in Surun'. It took me a moment to parse they were calling to me; I had forgotten all about my Surun' clothing. "Take a look at this fine honey crystal . . ."

It was a woman a decade younger than me. Someone I knew.

I turned away sharply and pushed my way through the crowd. Did she recognize me? I remembered her name now. Morit. Morit-nai-Niglah from the Morit oreg.

I was halfway to the edge of the square when she caught up with me. "Bashri? Bashri-nai-Tammah, is that you?"

Hearing my old name hurt. Hurt more sharply than I thought possible. I opened my mouth to correct her, closed it. Said instead, "How did you know?"

She giggled. "You always run around in men's clothing, though I've never yet seen you in Surun' men's clothing . . . It looks good on you."

I shrugged to conceal my confusion and pain. "I'll see you later, all right?"

Not waiting for an answer, I pushed through the crowd, dove through the narrow side streets as fast as I could.

I knew my way, and the special shape my deep-names could make to open the old rickety gate. It led down the stairs to another door, and more stairs beyond that, leading me underground.

The workshop below was lit by candlebulbs that floated under the ceiling, but the room itself was empty. Everyone was at market. My workbench appeared untouched, covered by an oiled tarpcloth.

I took off my veil and put it back in my pocket. Pulled the tarp down. My scrap metal and my tools were all intact, and the complex deepname ward I had installed before leaving had kept them free from rust. Touching the tools anchored me. Man or woman, I was the person who knew how to use them.

Uiziya needed a moving chair. I had no idea if she truly needed it. But I needed to make it for her. I had failed to heal Uiziya, failed in the first place to stop Benesret before she inflicted the wound. Because I believed Uiziya would betray me. I lacked trust, but I would not betray her now.

I picked up the metalcutter and made it move with my deepnames.

Uiziya e Lali

I came to. Didn't it always begin like this? There had been a physicker, and the shining grid of deepnames over my withered thigh. And words, his words in Iyari, which I could not understand. But the meaning was clear. He wanted a carpet that could be sold at market—no, not at market. Not sold. Given to someone.

Nen-sasaïr's voice, speaking rapidly, as if pleading. Darkness.

When I returned from it, I was alone. The room was empty, warm and perfumed with a heavy, cloying scent that made my eyes sting and water. Lily flowers, there at the corner.

The door opened, but in the frame, a net of shining deepname light glittered, stronger than any door. Behind the stinging light was a shadowed presence. A guardian of bones—Benesret herself, or someone like her. Perhaps my head was on fire and it was not Benesret. Just a person with bones under their skin.

"Aunt," I whispered, and my words reverberated off the old, stained alabaster ceiling, off the fabric-padded walls, echoing into harshness.

"What do you need?" the shadowed person asked.

I need a loom. A loom of bones, so I can weave on it. I was restless in my skin and spinning like yarn out of long, slow tugs of pain. *My flesh is not enough for you, Aunt. I need a loom so that I would weave on it a cloth of bones, and it will make you love me like you loved me when I was a little girl.*

"Where is your companion?" my aunt asked.

"I don't know." There was no trace of nen-sasaïr. Only his ward.

"Let me in, then."

"I cannot."

"Let me in. I love you. Let me in." My aunt said this. It had to be her.

I strained and twisted on the bed, crying until I could summon my deepnames, one-syllable and three-syllable, not very powerful but crafty. The Weaver's Promise. Nen-sasaïr's more powerful magical ward was not made to restrain me, just to keep people from entering the room. To keep my aunt away, and all the voices of the desert that called to me from all the bones in the world.

I made an opening in the ward so my aunt could come in, and she did. A second person was now at the door. It was my aunt again, dressed in white like an assassin.

My aunt, who was already inside, picked up the carpet of wanderlust. "Look," she said. "It is woven of sand." The carpet, blood-stained and weary, not much too look at, like me. "It is beautiful. What is it?"

"Don't you know? It is my carpet of wanderlust." I had once woven it with such yearning. The white bones gleaming in the weave symbolized birds in flight, for Bird herself to watch me in my peregrinations. "You taught me how to weave it." This close, I could see my aunt was not really my aunt but the physicker, come back to see me again.

"Perhaps you would be willing to part from it, to sell it?"

Yes, that was what the physicker wanted, that first

time when my head was too heavy with pain. "What I want is a loom," I said.

"You are in pain." The second, white-robed aunt stepped over the threshold now, past nen-sasaïr's torn and tattered ward. This wasn't my aunt, either. The new person spoke my language with a peculiar lilt, as if he was a neighbor from an encampment not too far away. "We will take you to where there is a loom."

"No, no." If I left, nen-sasaïr would lose me. He'd left a ward; he was coming back. That I knew. And I was in too much pain to move.

"Let me ease your pain," said the physicker.

"Where is my aunt?" I asked. *You were her, just a short time ago . . .*

A shallow bowl of warm liquid was tilted to my lips.

"Drink this, and we will take you to her."

I did not want to, but it spilled down my throat anyway, bitter and astringent, just like the potions nen-sasaïr made for me, only stronger.

"Careful," someone said. It was in Iyari. I did not understand much. "If she can . . . she can truly weave this weave . . . the master . . ."

The warm, deep darkness wove itself again.

THE FOUR PROFOUND WEAVES

nen-sasaïr

I kept working on Uiziya's chair. It would be neither big nor clumsy. It would be lightweight. It would be collapsible into a staff, which would help stabilize and support Uiziya when she was ready to walk again. A tricky design, but thinking about it made me calmer. I worked, not noticing much, until noise and commotion came from outside, and could not be ignored.

I lifted my head. Many voices and footsteps. I heard the withdrawal of air and an exhalation, as from many throats flowed forth greetings, cries of "Bashri! You are back!" and women rushing forward to embrace me.

I raised my hand to put a stop to all of it. "I am not Bashri. I never was. I am a man, and travel as nen-sasaïr."

"You are no man," laughed someone. "You just like men's clothes—we know you!"

"Grief is hard," said another. "It hasn't been a year since Bashri-nai-Leylit was taken up by Bird—grief is hard, my friend." She too had lost a lover last year, I remembered. "But you are Bashri-nai-Tammah, artificer and trader . . ."

I shook my head. "No. I went to the desert and changed my body."

"Grief does strange things to people, but still . . ."

Another woman spoke. "If I fashion a beak from

91

my deepnames and make it stick to my face, it will not make me Bird. *You* are a woman of the Khana, doing womanly things, you are doing rebellious womanly things—that's why you are here, in the underground workshop . . ."

"I am making a moving chair for my friend," I said.

The speaker continued. "If you were a man, you would be making your chair on the men's side of the quarter, behind the white walls, where artifice is permitted—you would not be a woman rebel with us all those years . . ."

I said wearily, "We all did manly things, but out of all of you, I alone transformed my body. This is not about artifice for me, or trade, or childbirth, or whatever it is Khana women do which is traditional or rebellious—no, this is about what feels right for me."

"Hush," said another voice. My erstwhile mentor Sulikhah-nai-Tali, who was older than me by almost three decades. By the virtue of her great age, she was the sole survivor of her oreg, and so we called her simply Sulikhah. She was our workshop's leader, and now she spoke. "Women, we are here because we are rebels, because we have always been rebels. Bashri-nai-Tammah had been a rebel among us, making with us works of artifice forbidden to women. Let her work."

"I am not Bashri," I said. "It is exactly because you cannot hold my truth that I had to go away, among Bird-eaters, no—among non-Khana . . ." My tongue was slipping. I did not want to call Uiziya and her people Bird-eaters, even though they ate the flesh of birds and animals forbidden to us.

"Finish your chair," Sulikhah said.

They all stood there and watched as I worked. I would have preferred they didn't all stare—it made me feel even more an outsider than when I entered the quarter in secret and veiled. It was too painful to contemplate what they thought of me. But I had to continue my work.

When the staff was finished, Sulikhah took me out of the workshop, and into the deepest night.

"You can stay here," she said. "And we can keep talking, but if you stay here, everybody will see you as a woman, as Bashri, no matter what body you now have."

"I am nen-sasaïr." The pain of being called Bashri again and again lacerated me. I needed a real name to outweigh all the Bashris, my two lost lovers and my past tormented, hidden self. I needed a Khana name. Why had I ever felt otherwise? Benesret was right that she could not help me.

But who would give me a Khana man's name? These women, who Bashried me until I could scream?

Sulikhah spoke. "Long time ago . . ."

Then nothing.

I wanted to move faster, but I matched my pace to her halting steps. She did not touch me as we walked through the warmth of narrow nighttime streets.

"Long time ago," she said again, after a while, "I had a lover like you. A lover who was born and raised among us on the women's side of the quarter, but who had always been a man."

I stopped. "What happened to him?" I had needed his tale desperately, before—and now, too. And yet I'd never heard of such a thing. I'd always felt alone here, where these tales—these tales existed, stories of people like me, but hushed so that we could not learn about each other.

"What happened to him?" I repeated, like Uiziya would have done in my place.

Sulikhah did not answer or stop, and after a moment, I followed her once again. We reached the inner wall, and the chiseled white stones of the men's inner quarter now glowed, radiant with flickers of deepname lights.

"In the end, we traveled to Che Mazri. To the Old Royal's court." Sulikhah had swallowed parts of this tale. "To the Sandbird Festival. The Old Royal helped him transform."

Sulikhah led me along the wall. She fell silent again, and her garments made swishing sounds as she walked. "We came back in secret."

We stopped by a round door of blackened iron. It was elaborate and old, reinforced with bindings of enameled white metal and precious stone—emerald and sapphire and ruby, the crowning jewels of our desert trade. In the middle of the door was a lock-shaping made like a cloud of interlocking white metal swirls, each hammered precisely with the tiny letters of the writ.

"I took him here," Sulikhah said. "He made a key out of the Birdseed writ, and walked in." She took a steadying breath. "I will wait for you here, as I waited for him."

"What happened to him?" My voice rang heavy with yearning.

"He never came out."

And she smiled.

I put my hand on the lock.

Was that the hope I sought so many decades, wandering in men's clothing between the narrow streets of the quarter, hoping one day to be myself without knowing that my dearest love could not love me if I changed? What would I have done if Bashri-nai-Leylit had brought me here forty years ago, when I was young and full of hope and vigor?

Bashri-nai-Leylit could have done this for me. She could have brought me here, then stood and waited. Could have smiled.

Under my hand, I felt the ancient deepnames of the ward stir awake and examine me. Then the ward swirled in my vision, forming columns upon columns of letters of the Birdseed writ. I could use my deepnames to sort them, to find a way in. Here was a squiggle-seed for *daled*, a door. *Yated*, wedge. The letters combined and split, each possessing a value of numbers as well as of sounds. I could make them all dance, then push at the yielding mass of iron and enter the streets of the inner quarter.

I would be among men.

Among scholars.

I had dreamt of this day so many times, ever since I was little. I dreamt of running through one of these gates unnoticed, as a child, sneaking in before my grandmothers could stop me. I would hide among the narrow streets of men, unseen until I learned how to better pass among them. I would sneak into the holy rooms where boys my age learned the writ. I would become a ghost, learning the writ in secret while the boys slept.

Later, after Benesret's promise, returning from the desert with the small cloth of winds in my hands, I began to fantasize about entering the gate not as a ghost, but as a man who had a right to be there. And that was when my mind would hiccup and withdraw, for how would I prove—how would I fit—even having the right body, but not the lifetime of learning, how would I fit on the men's side?

Still now, letter by letter, I moved the puzzle, combining it into a line from the Books of Birdseed I knew by heart. The words of the dawnsong.

The dawn is never far away.

The letters spun under my hand, showing me the vision of what awaited inside. A chamber of holy immersion, a ritual bath where I would shed my profane clothing and immerse myself in the water gathered from sky-given rains, to purify myself from the dust and hassle of the outside world, to step truly then into the garments of holiness. I would not be questioned about my body and its iterations, but be accepted as all those who walked through the door were accepted. I would grow out my beard and wear Khana men's clothes. They would give me an artificer's tools—ancient and true and held by many hands before me—and I would make holy automata with the others. At dawn, I would lift my voice in song to Kimri.

I thought I heard his voice then; Kimri, Bird's hidden brother, the god of my people's men, locked away from the dirt and the noise and distraction of the outside world so that nothing would sully the song.

And I heard it, that song, like a surging wave of the rainbow washing the sky in the colors of jewels and of carpets—the red of madder and the yellow-sweet of weld, then indigo and walnut and emerald, turquoise and pink tourmaline. It was hope. My hope, and the hope of all others of my people who sang it throughout the landmass. The hope that wherever we gathered, wherever we wandered, exiled and unwanted, the dawn would still come for us. We only had to hold on.

What was I hoping for? What had I been holding out for, these forty years? This, a personal triumph, a withdrawal from the world. I had liberated myself from the strictures of my youth, and all my lovers were dead. My grandchildren fended for themselves. I could do what I wanted. I could go in.

Was this what I truly wanted?

While I struggled with myself, the melody surged—the dawnsinger's prayer, which is sung from the roof of the great gathering-place in the men's inner quarter, the song that is heard in the deadest hour of the night. That melody is as ancient as the landmass. It had accompanied my people when we were exiled from our ancient home, from the mountainous land of Keshet. The Khana men sang it, so the legend went, on our great peregrination north to Iyar. Powerful women formed an outer ring. Blessed by the goddess Bird, these women protected the men and the children from enemies and ambush and wild beasts, from all disasters which, raging, come into the world. Walking the road of our exile, shielded by our strongest women, the scholars sang to Kimri, as they sang now from the rooftops of the quarter.

"The dawn is never far away. The dawn is never far away."

Was this the hope I wanted? To walk in, forget the outside world, to cleanse its taint and dust from my body?

I raised my left hand to join my right, on the lock, and the wide staff I had made rattled out of my grip.

Uiziya.

Uiziya was outside, injured, in the hostel. I had

promised the physicker that I would come back after the Khana men sang.

If I were to go in and never come out, what would happen to my friend? She knew nobody, did not know the language of Iyar . . . she was wounded.

She was not even Khana.

I snatched my hands away from the lock.

"The lock recognized you as a man, I saw. But you could not solve it?" asked Sulikhah.

"No, no, it was easy. I solved it. I just did not turn it all the way." I took a breath. "But I need to go back. I cannot leave my companion, for she is sick and helpless."

Sulikhah looked at me, her eyes shrouded. "And this is the nature of women. Always given too much to those in our care."

"I am not a woman."

She shrugged. "You were brought up to be one. These things are hard to erase, much as you change otherwise."

This is not the nature of women, but rather the nature of all people who care. Uiziya had told me this once. "You can choose to care or not, and that is what people do."

Sulikhah shrugged again. "As you wish."

It had been better, coming here, than the fears my brain had spun. They did not accept me, but neither did they throw me out of the quarter. Help had been rendered to me despite argument. And yet, the only way to be truly myself was to abandon my friend and go inside. Make being a man among my people's men my only hope.

Above us, the dawnsong quieted down.

I placed my hand once again on the lock. Not because I wanted to turn it, but because I wanted, for the last brief moment, to see the ritual bath just behind the gate. To hear the lapping of water inside. To smell the rainwater that filled it.

Faintly, like a rustle that emerges from behind a curtain of noise, I heard a soft, reverberating sound—not of the rainwater, but of song. It was like the dawnsong, but more profound and at once subtler, hovering at the very edge of my senses. That, too, tapered off to a whisper, and then to nothing.

With a sigh, I stepped back.

I retrieved my staff-chair, and Sulikhah led me out of the quarter safely, for she was a woman given too much to those in her care.

IV.
DEATH

THE
RAINBOW-TIERED
COURT

nen-sasaïr

I was still on time. The hostel loomed dark in the deadest of pre-dawn darkness that stifled the magical lights and even the stars. The flowers that closed for the night did not yet begin to reopen. But something felt different here. I wanted to run—either forward or away—and yet I continued to approach at a steady pace, my feet knowing what my mind yet refused to acknowledge—that something was profoundly, irreparably amiss.

Uiziya was inside. I could not run away.

I drew on my deepnames and formed a protective construct, then entered the building. Up the stairs. Second floor. An enfilade of rooms, cloth-swaddled, smelling stale and treacherous in the gloom.

This was the door to the room where I left Uiziya—I had warded it—

The magic of my ward was in tatters.

With my senses enhanced hundredfold by the

powerful magic I wielded, I sensed three people in the room. And none of them breathed like Uiziya.

She was gone.

In a moment of vision I saw myself fleeing all the way back to the quarter. To the lock. The door to the innermost domain. I would be safe there, safe and serene and among my own.

But back when I still lived among Khana women, my powerful magic made me one of them. Three deepnames is the most a mind can hold, and my configuration was recognized as a powerful woman's magic to use for protection, for trade; the men had subtler and weaker configurations. In all our stories of exile, women walked in an outer circle, protecting those who walked within. I could now choose to walk within and be protected by others.

My thoughts jumbled, confused by myself, the inner and outer circles mixed and tangled. I did not know how to make my thoughts come right, but I would not desert Uiziya. Perhaps it was my upbringing, or perhaps it was simply me.

I clutched Uiziya's white staff—her collapsed chair I had made—and lit the white enamel surface of it with my magic. I stepped into the abandoned room, closing my eyes as I made the staff flash with a sudden, dazzling light.

The soldiers threw themselves at me, half-blinded, screaming. One had a two-deepname configuration, and the others had scimitars curved and polished, but the shield of my deepnames, and the staff's light, had bought me a moment. I lunged, the staff too light-weight and inconsequential in my hands.

Uiziya e Lali

A story floated like stars in the darkness that pulsed with the insistence of pain. I would catch them one by one, all the diamondflies my aunt had made, and I would know again the truth of the wide-open skies where the ancient wind meanders from sandwave to sandwave, revealing and hiding its secrets.

I will teach you the last of my secrets, my aunt never said to me.

There was no wind. I was under a ceiling, low and fashioned of stone, each boulder enormous like a heaving belly pregnant with my death. I was a Su-run' woman from the tents, not used to stone rooms crushing me. Squeezing me in. Even my carpet of sand was gone.

"Look up," somebody said.

In front of me there I saw bars, thick with iron and magic. Beyond the bars, a corridor of stone. And then I saw an elaborate enameled birdcage, barely contained in the corridor.

Inside that birdcage was a man.

He was ancient and stooped like my aunt, but not my aunt. Dressed in blue robes embroidered in blue, decorated with beads of sapphire and lapis, turquoise and aquamarine. His brown skin, just slightly lighter than mine, was wrinkled and spotted in very great age, but his eyes were as dark and agile as a youngster's. His long, scraggly beard was oiled and painted indigo-black. On his head he wore a circlet of sapphires.

Three other people flanked the birdcage and propped the corridor wall. The physicker, who had told me to look up. An assassin in white robes that smelled like my aunt's tent of bones. Another person, whose magic roiled off their skin. Such great excess, barely contained. In one hand that person held a whip of braided leather. In the other hand, an iron rod of full faces, leering and leering and leering at me.

All were silent.

"Why am I here?" The pain of my body felt less sharp now. Still present like a lover, but less demanding.

The roiling magical person lashed out with his whip, tearing at me. The pain was hot and fast, a relief from all my other pain, and then the new pain was terrible too. I doubled up on the ground, and because of the motion, my wilted leg sent horrible jolts up my torso, overcoming the pain from the whip, moving putrid and slow toward my heart.

My tormentor said, "Speak when you're spoken to!"

"Desist, my dear torturer," the man in the birdcage said. "I need her in one piece. What is left of her, anyway." My Iyari was very poor, but I could understand this, not just from words, but his gestures, his tone.

The old man in the birdcage turned to me next. "You had woven a carpet from sand." He spoke in Iyari, and the physicker translated.

Who are you? But I knew without asking. The Ruler of Iyar was rumored to move around in a birdcage throne, and he was very old.

"I lost that carpet," I said, biding for time.

"Oh no, you have not." He smiled, and his teeth glinted like Benesret's palisade of bones. "I have already examined it, already acquired it, already put it away."

You acquired it? Acquired without my consent to the trade? Acquired without even paying me? I did not say it, but it must have shown on my face, because he said, "Do you know that it is forbidden for a woman to openly bear her deepnames here, nomad?"

He made a motion, and the torturer's whip lashed me on the leg that had wilted. I did not even scream.

"I took your carpet in compensation for your crime."

The physicker added, after translating, some words of his own. "Our sovereign has been exceedingly patient with you. I would advise you not to overextend his patience."

Yes. This was the Ruler of Iyar, the Collector. Here, in an underground dungeon, talking to me.

"Now, tell me about it," the Collector said. "Your carpet of sand."

All out of subterfuge, I obeyed. "I wove the carpet out of the desert's flesh, so it would take me where I wished to go."

"Hmm." He steepled his hands together, as if deep in thought. "My people heard you say that you are familiar with a legendary desert weave, a carpet made of death and death alone. Is that so?"

I will teach you to weave from death, my aunt never told me. She promised she would, but she never did.

I spoke out, my voice dry and brittle like the white curls of Benesret's hair. "You already possess the greatest treasure ever woven. Why do you need a carpet made of death?"

The torturer lifted the rod. I could see it closer now; it was forged of iron and molded with screaming faces as dark as the iron was dark. He inhaled and imbued the iron with deepnames so furious that the faces screamed themselves red. Then he swung it.

The rod stopped just a breath away from my cheek, so hot that I tried to pull away. The motion made my bad leg convulse. Where was nen-sasaïr? He had left me. Everybody leaves. My aunt had left me, and Lali, and my children, and nen-sasaïr—all the screaming faces in the iron. But I would prove myself to Benesret.

The Ruler of Iyar waited for me to live through my pain, a benevolent smile on his face. The torturer looked hungry. The assassin, attentive. The physicker, blank.

The Ruler of Iyar said, "You made that old carpet from sand. More of a rag, and yet it had a certain charm. Is it your only bid at this craft?"

"I wove it forty years ago," I said, bristling, "under the guidance of my aunt, who made the greatest treasure ever woven. The carpet of song. You have it, here, somewhere."

"Ah," he said, his eyes bright and predatory in that wilted face, burning like they burned when he had watched my pain. "So did she teach you?"

The fourth and last mystery of the ever-changing desert is a weave of bones: you have learned it, and now you are ready to put together my loom.

My aunt had never said this to me.

Despite myself, because of myself, I forced the words out again. "Why do you need it?"

"I sent emissaries to the desert court of my enemy the Old Royal, spies and traders to the Maiva'at and the Gehezi, to the many-folded realms of Lepaleh in the south, to the Mon Mountains in the farthest east. Again and again I sent emissaries to your own people, the Surun'. For forty years I sought a new

109

woven treasure to equal the carpet woven from song. I have not found it."

The physicker translated all that, while I thought, *you roamed far and wide to avoid my question.* "Why do you need it?" I asked again, louder, for I had a habit of repeating myself until I was satisfied.

The torturer raised his rod of faces, but the Ruler of Iyar ordered him to step back. Then he spoke. "You are nothing, and nothing arises from dirt to fashion the treasure I hold. Then to dirt you shall return, while my treasure lives on. Why must you question me?"

"You, too, shall return to dirt," I said, averting my gaze from the torturer's grimace. "So why do you need it?"

"I shall not return to dirt, old woman, for I did not come from it." His face lost some of its anger. "You think that because we must die, we must care about nothing? The older we get, the less we should care?"

I turned from him, shamed. "No."

"Change is the world's greatest danger. Around the world you and others, old woman, chafe at my rule, forever desiring a change, yet change destroys all. If not for that power of change, we would not need to die. But you people do not understand. You rebel, you wander from place to place, you chafe at my rule, thinking that something else, somewhere else, would be better. It isn't. But I save you. I am the one who is centered and stable, anchoring the whole world from my rainbow-tiered court, unmoved by world's wildness, contained in my birdcage throne. The best of the world comes to me, and I save it from change and I save it from you, who know only dirt even as you make treasure. The treasure is only safe in my palace. Separated from your stench and squalor, forever locked in my coffers. Are you satisfied?"

I was not quite satisfied. I did not fully understand his answer; but it was an answer. "Yes," I said.

"I sent emissaries to your aunt, when your people exiled her. She told me she'll weave from death. A treasure greater than her treasure of song. A treasure that will complete me. But she had not done it. She failed."

I had always thought that of all of them, Benesret only abandoned me because she loved me. She did not want to feed on me when I was young. Because she loved me. Instead, she had fed on other people in secret, and then on my husband Lali, but Lali did not love me like she did. So I found her. Told her, *take what you need from me.* And she did.

And then she abandoned me again.

Nothing matters. But I can put together my own loom, now. Make my own profound weave.

My lips moved, disgorging words I did not know I wanted to say. "I am better than her."

"Yes?" hissed the Ruler of Iyar.

"I can weave you one better than hers," I said. A

treasure made out of death, which would transcend her, devour even my own need for her love.

"Then weave me that carpet," he said, "And I will let you go, and pay you lavishly." But I heard the lie as it dripped, poison-sweet, from his lips.

"I am old and have lived a life," I said. I had wanted to live, or perhaps I did not. It was hard to know, now, after my aunt fed on me. Life and death were blurred in my mind, in the underground palace. Perhaps it did not matter. I knew this: I needed a loom.

"I will weave for you," I said. "But on two conditions. The first is to see my aunt's great carpet of song, so I can learn to surpass it. The second is bones. Bones to weave from, and bones to make me a loom."

The Ruler of Iyar laughed, a short, sweet, satisfied sound. "Bones, my dear, I have here in abundance. Come, I will show you."

The torturer and the physicker moved forward to drag me out, the pain almost dulling my eyes again. Almost. Out of the corner of my eye, I watched the assassin watch me. His white clothes smelled like my aunt's skin.

The Four Profound Weaves

nen-sasaïr

I bound the two unconscious soldiers with my magic. They wouldn't stay that way for long, and I was winded, but my anger had carried me through. The third of the men, semi-conscious, kneeling, stared up at me. His eyes were glazed in shock.

"Where is Uiziya?" I wheezed. The darkness and dust of the room strained my breathing. My arms trembled, and something twitched again and again in my face.

"Who?" the man asked, recoiling from me.

"The woman who was here. The one who was injured." It was all my fault. My foot prodded what remained of my staff-chair. I had fashioned it with such hope, in the quarter. Now it was broken. Discarded. I'd left Uiziya alone and in danger, for this. For my vanity.

"Where is she?"

"I don't know, man. Taken to the palace."

A terrible fear bloomed in me. Perhaps it was rage. "To the palace? What for?"

The guard recoiled in earnest, his arms and legs making little useless motions on the garish carpet. "To the master. Don't kill me!"

"I won't." But my magic seized him and hoisted him up like a rag doll. My legs nearly buckled. I would not sustain this for long. I was not in my prime, and I hadn't slept. But for now, the power of my rare three-deepname configuration upheld me. "You will take me there."

The man mumbled something. I did not listen.

Was she taken alive? But life and death had no meaning in the lowest levels of the Rainbow-Tiered Court. In the dungeons, life and its end are mated like two royal swans, their necks winding round and round each other. I was not sure if the guard spoke, or my brain spun the words for me out of the stifling, stale darkness.

I kicked the bent remains of my staff even farther away. Wrapped myself, instead, in an unconscious soldier's coat. I wanted to pick up his scimitar, to wrap my fingers around its leather-wrapped handle as if it was Uiziya's staff. My staff. My handiwork. I lied to myself that I wanted to ease her life—perhaps I had wanted to simply to steer her this way and that like I had with Bashri-nai-Leylit. And so I had not protected Uiziya when she needed me most.

I left the scimitar alone. It wasn't my weapon. My deepnames would either suffice or they wouldn't.

I pushed the soldier out of the room. Out of the back exit, into the familiar, scented night.

"Bring me there."

The Four Profound Weaves

Uiziya e Lali

I had been delirious, I now recognized. Delirious on Benesret's diamondflies. They sucked life from my blood, and fed Benesret; but I was her niece, and my blood and her blood were alike, and so her predation had fed me in turn. We were tied, she and I, connected by her theft of my life and by my withered flesh. She took, but she gave, too: perhaps without knowing. Perhaps she had learned from her teacher, whom I had never met, or from the Orphan itself, that desperate star underneath the School of Assassins. It did not matter now. Inside me I could almost hear my bones rattle, whispering truths I had not known before Benesret took from me. I listened to the speech of my withered leg, telling me of a loom which was made of bones. The bones in all the stories. The bones that have a story to tell, a story that persists beyond the last breath and demands to be told.

I could weave from death now, if I put my hands to a loom.

The physicker and the torturer dragged me out of the cell. I do not remember how the Ruler of Iyar moved in his cage; I was overwhelmed with a new feeling. I was listening to bones.

Because now the bones of my death-withered leg called to bones I could sense through the thickness of stone walls around me, through the floors leading deeper down. Beyond the thickness of these impenetrable walls, through the dense body of the earth, my sense of bones stretched up, bloomed like the bones of murdered brides that played pipe and reedflute to leery passersby. My sense of bones grew upward through the earth, bloomed into the city's nighttime air to sense all the dead of Iyar, and beyond them—those drowned at sea, and beyond. The world's grief, singing for me to be spun and woven.

And back into the earth my sense of bones plunged, through the many layers of the palace. If all of the world's forsaken deaths were weeds, this place was a garden tenderly tended. I sensed how the palace was thick with death, below, beyond, between. In all directions, death had taken a root here. In the Collector's palace, where change was not allowed, it was death that endured. And I was getting closer to where it sang the loudest.

We stopped by an iron door. It was simple, without adornment, barred and locked with a lock with a young woman's terrified face. The Ruler of Iyar made a motion with his hand, and the lock screamed and split open.

The door swung inward, revealing a stale reek of darkness, within which nothing could be seen.

The Four Profound Weaves

nen-sasaïr

The walk to the palace was not very long, but I was
on my last breath, the weight of my guilt and my age
and the sleeplessness of the night binding my feet as
if with weighted chains. I drew on my magic to give
myself some nourishment, energy. This, too, was dangerous
and hard to do safely with all but the most
stable configurations, of which mine was one. I was
lucky, but even so, I knew this action would sap me.
I would be paying for this in the days to come, but it
would be a worry for later. If I survived.

The guard had taken me to a row of buildings beyond
a tall arch of chiseled roses and swans of gray
stone that loomed shadow-deep in the predawn
darkness.

"Get me in," I hissed to my captive, "or die," and
my magic prodded him. He took me through the
arch, but not into any of the public entrances to these
buildings. We walked through a narrow, dark alley,
down a long spiral run of stairs, down into a well of
stone that led to an even smaller door, with no decoration
or signs. The guard pushed it through, and
we entered.

Pitch darkness. Not a sound. The guard at my
side breathed heavily, and I knew he was plotting
something. I took a deep breath, and as I pulled on
my deepnames to create a light and still hold on to
my prisoner, the Bird-forsaken son of filth tripped

me with his foot, and my grip on him slipped. I fell. I fell and fell, down the stairs, into the maw of unlife and no-light.

Above me, I heard the guard's cry, more terrified than gleeful. "If you follow the path, it will lead you to the master. To your fate."

I had no time for him. Rolling down, I fought hard to keep the hold on my deepnames and dampen my fall—enough to survive unbroken, not enough to stop or slow my descent.

Far above now, the sound of a door slammed shut.

Uiziya e Lali

The physicker drew back from the gaping door. The Ruler of Iyar contemplated the physicker's bloodless face. "What are you afraid of . . . ?"

"This place. I did not know—"

At a sign from the Ruler of Iyar, the assassin prodded the physicker forward. The assassin's robes smelled slightly of damp and of Benesret's skin, and I knew that my aunt had woven this fabric.

"You can stay outside," said the Ruler of Iyar to the assassin.

The assassin spoke. "I will follow you wherever you go."

THE FOUR PROFOUND WEAVES

They say in the desert that assassins are orphans. Many are and many are not, but they are alone and unwanted by others, even by themselves. That's how the Headmaster recruits them, and then he trains them to be loyal. They would follow their masters wherever they wished to go. Even into the roiling domain of death. Just like I had followed Benesret.

The Ruler of Iyar now spoke to the physicker. "I need a translator." But I understood him. I did not know how my understanding had grown, and it was strange. I did not reveal it.

"You must come with me," said the Ruler of Iyar.

Blood flowed away from the physicker's face, and he swayed on his feet. "Please . . . my sovereign . . ."

The assassin pushed him into the darkness beyond the door. Then he picked me up, and carried me over the threshold into utter darkness. It no longer terrified me, because from it voices whispered to me, begged me in this Iyari tongue and in nen-sa-saïr's native Khanishti, and in all the tongues of the desert. They whispered and called and threatened and pleaded, but I could not quite attend to their speech yet. The birdcage throne of the Ruler of Iyar floated in, and the iron door closed.

The torturer remained outside.

It was dark among the whispers, but the birdcage throne lit up with bluish deepname lights, casting shadows over a vast, cavernous space. It was full. Full of skulls and finger bones and thigh bones and ribcages as far as the eye could see. Between the human bones I saw smaller skeletons. I recognized sandbirds—I never thought that they died—their long curved beaks of bone and long, long legs. I saw many smaller bird skeletons, too—long-legged and short-legged, with wide beaks, with narrow beaks. Feathers and flesh would tell me their names, but all that remained was bones.

I could not support my weight, and so the assassin carried me, breathing heavily with the effort. We moved upon a narrow path among the bones.

"Most people know," said the old man in the birdcage throne, "that I thirst for great works of art from the farthest corners of the world, for they nourish my spirit, and I am nourished, too, by the knowledge that they would be safe in my care. Few know that I have a second collection. I do not like for either to be seen."

The physicker translated, but many of the words were lost, mumbled and swallowed in his fear. I waited for the translation to conclude before giving a nod. The assassin's fingers dug into my arms in his effort to hold me.

"Wild peoples outside of the city allow their women to bear deepnames," said the Ruler of Iyar. "But here in Iyar we are better. We know that women given magical power are born for distinction, but they have holier tasks than magical geometry."

The physicker translated his words.

Yes, we learned this, the desert over: in the springflower city of Iyar, women with magical ability were praised as brides; they married well and could live richly, but always at a price of their power. We wondered sometimes, in the desert, why they didn't all leave. It seemed so strange for us that they would accept their fates when freedom awaited outside of the city.

But I had not left my place either. I sat immovable for forty years before I could muster the will to do something. Nen-sasaïr waited, too, for forty years, to go through his ritual. It is only in stories that change is easily found.

The Ruler of Iyar spoke again. "Attending to one's husband, ornamenting his honor, the birthing and rearing of children, the smooth running of the household—those are the acts of a civilized woman. Certainly, even in the great Burri desert, you heard."

I waited for the physicker to translate, then spoke. "I heard."

"But some of our women," the Collector continued. "Some are rebels."

He swung his arm higher, letting the light of his magic snatch mountains of bones from the dark's domain, then return them to darkness as his hand moved on. "Look how beautifully they shine. I will leave you a light for your loom, and you will weave from these women, my dear, weave for me a carpet made of death. And thus shall my two collections meet in a treasure which will surpass all."

The physicker shook through the translation. I did not think he would last much longer.

Supported by the solidity of the assassin's grip, I spoke. "I asked you to take me first to see my aunt's carpet, so that I will learn to surpass it."

"No," the Ruler of Iyar said. "I do not want your artistry to be contaminated by its screeching. If you please me with the weave, then you may indeed see it, and know that you have surpassed her."

The voices of the bones were louder now, talking. Questioning me. I needed to be alone with them. I needed to sit.

I said, "I am satisfied."

The Ruler of Iyar nodded, and the assassin stepped forward, shifting me in his arms. The motion twisted me, long and horrible. Twitching in pain, I saw a long blade glint in the assassin's hand. He split the physicker's throat without letting me fall, without sullying his garments, or me.

The physicker toppled onto the white domain of bone.

"He was not one of us," the Ruler of Iyar simply. "And so he had seen too much."

I did not answer. I was barely able to breathe. And I was not supposed to understand.

The Collector left a small light for me, and made the throne float out through the opening.

The assassin remained behind. With me, in this treasury of death, by the newly dead and the old.

"Find for me a place that is not bone," I said to him in Surun'. "For I must begin my preparations, and I will not sit on my sisters."

He found such a place for me, and lowered me down, with my back away from the door. My face toward the shuddering whispers.

nen-sasaïr

My body wasn't broken. The structure I had created had dampened my fall. But I was badly bruised, and almost crying out from the pain. My legs folded under me. In the darkness, I stretched out my hand and touched old dry stone; the weight of the earth pressed below and above. I had to have light, but it took me ages to summon even a single deepname. Shaking with fatigue and pain, I lit a candlebulb, a small ball-shaped light. The first magic one learns in childhood: the easiest, the quickest, the kindest.

The candlebulb floated just above me, illuminating a tunnel of dark gray stone. To my right, I saw a narrow, circular opening in the wall. I had come through there—down the narrow, sharp stairs. I climbed up, however long it took, I would perhaps emerge again in the streets of Iyar.

Uiziya. I had to find Uiziya.

I clambered to my feet. I felt battered, unsteady. The dull aches in my spine radiated all through my torso, but I forced myself to move forward. I should have made the moving chair for myself, not for Uiziya. Maybe.

My hands squeezed into fists. It was as if I was still holding the handles of Bashri-nai-Leylit's chair as she sat, no longer well enough to steer it with her deepnames. I wanted—what had I wanted then? Some control, like she had over me all my life. Control over movement, for hadn't she told me, *Don't leave me. I do not want you to go. You cannot be a man.*

Don't change.

And I did not want to lose her, so I stayed until death had loosened our grip on each other. But now I betrayed Uiziya, because either gripping or leaving was all that I knew.

I walked forward for what felt like hours. The underground maze of stone corridors held me, and perhaps it did not matter if I moved at all. I was here, neither dead nor alive, and my motion or stillness did not change anything. I could as well stop and lie down on the floor.

There was chalk underfoot—I'd just noticed—and the stone walls here were marked with names, and yet more and more names, as I followed them. The names of all the rebels—the women who dared bear deepnames in the springflower city of Iyar. Laaguti Birdwing, the most famous rebel of them all, who broke out of the palace dungeons with a small handful of other prisoners; the rebels escaped these walls and fled Iyar in a ship, sailing into the wests unknown. I read her name out loud, and then the names of her friends, scribbled in the same old, large curving script. And then even more names, in newer scripts of Iyar. I walked forward, reading them under my breath. Were some of these rebels changers, like me? In-betweeners, like my grandchild Kimi? Would I ever know? Why were their names written here?

I touched one of the names, brought the chalk to my lips, expecting it to be bitter. But I felt no taste, for my gaze fell upon one name in particular. It wasn't in Iyari, but in Khanishti, the language of the quarter, curving and small like the Birdseed writ. The name of my lover who perished under the weight of the palace.

Bashri-nai-Divrah.

She had been barely twenty. All three of us had been so young when we first formed our oreg and became lovers. Bashri-nai-Divrah had gone out of the quarter to trade. In concession to our faith and custom, Khana women were permitted to keep their deepnames outside the quarter, in Iyar, if they were properly veiled. But the trade that Bashri-nai-Divrah was invited to had been a ruse. Her veil had been torn away by her tormentors, and that was considered her crime.

The Ruler of Iyar took Bashri-nai-Divrah, and the two of us could buy her life back with the greatest treasure ever woven. Except that when we returned with it, she was already dead.

I had to move on, but I could not bear leaving. But something had changed in the air.

I turned away from the wall and saw ghosts.

At first, I thought my eyes were deceiving me. Bubbles of soft white floated around, filling the narrow corridor. They had no bodies, just faces, each screaming itself wide open. A young man. An old man. Two older women. A younger woman. A child.

They all had sharp teeth, and all of them wailed soundlessly, circling me. I tried to summon my deep-names, to push the bubbles away, but a voice came out of the darkness of the corridor ahead. *If you attack them with magic, they'll tear you apart.*

A man emerged, and I recognized him from many whispered descriptions, the legends of fear. The royal torturer with his iron rod. The faces in it he commanded to tear and bite at his victims; the faces ate flesh and drank the souls of his victims; the faces always obeyed his will out of love.

The torturer lifted his rod. "Come on," he called to the ghosts. "We found the intruder. It's time to go home."

The older ghosts flowed into the rod. It had appeared smooth just a moment ago, but now it grew chiseled faces. As one, the faces began to scream, their iron mouths opening and closing.

The ghost of the younger man grimaced, but followed the others into the rod. The child still circled me, wild-eyed, sharp-toothed. I heard its voice, as loud as if it was in my head.

IT HURTS

"Juma!" The torturer called. "Come here! Juma!"

IT HURTS IT HURTS IT HURTS IT HURTS

The child floated around me as I searched frantically for something to say. *I met your friend out above—a friend who worried about you—is this man your father?*

The child ghost floated, reluctantly, finally, into the rod, just as guards caught up with the torturer. I was too dizzy from shock and pain to resist.

Uiziya e Lali

I had grown into my pain, sitting immovably among my sisters. By the door, the assassin was still. The light my captor left had fizzled out, and I was attending to darkness. One by one, the bones spoke to me, telling the stories of the women they had been.

An ancient voice emerged first, with a singsong, elegant cadence. *"I was proud to become one of Laaguti's rebels.*" I wanted to hear more of this story, but then another voice distracted me.

"*Children,*" another voice came. An Iyari voice, it sounded old-fashioned, but not as ancient. "*I could no longer care for my beautiful children. After my deepnames were destroyed, I fell into despair . . . they became name-orphans, wandering the streets . . .*"

And I heard another Iyari voice, quiet and plaintive. "*I waited for Bird to take me, but she did not come for me—she did not come for any of us, so our souls were stranded here . . .*"

I wanted more time to think about these stories, to remember what stories I heard in my youth, to ask the bones questions, but I could not. I had to attend to the dead, attend quietly while hundreds of voices emerged all around me, attend as well as I could.

A Khana voice, young, its lilting tones reminding me of Bashri-nai-Leylit when I met her decades ago. "*. . . I ventured out of the quarter . . .*"

A voice from the desert came next, not snake-Surun' but in the cadence of one of our neighboring encampments. "*One and three syllables make the Maker's Angle, which in the desert is called the Weaver's Promise—I did not know that as a woman I was not allowed to carry magic in Iyar . . .*"

A deep Iyari voice. "*. . . so I kept my deepnames in secret. I did not want to rebel, I just wanted to keep making art . . .*"

"*. . . she made glass sculptures, these big multicol-*

ored birds . . ." another voice echoed. "*You need two deepnames to make the glass sing, she taught me in secret . . .*"

"*. . . and then they came for us . . .*"

I kept turning my head as the bones told their stories, attending, remembering. From farther away in the darkness another Khana voice came, older-sounding than the first. "*I am a woman, but I wanted to sing, my deepnames lifting up my voice—to sing to Bird . . .*"

The voices spoke faster now, pushing tightly together like threads on a loom, and I could no longer distinguish among them.

"*. . . because we needed to eat . . .*"

"*. . . I think Bird came looking for us, but she could not find us . . .*"

"*. . . a Khana woman can keep her deepnames in Iyar if she is properly veiled . . .*"

"*. . . Bird could not find us—for he has locked this place away from Bird . . .*"

"*. . . I want my children back . . . I want my magic back . . .*"

"*. . . I'd kill him for this, I'd tear him apart . . .*"

"*. . . of the throng of us, Laaguti managed to escape with only a handful of others, sailed west and beyond the sea, but we were recaptured and tried . . .*"

"*. . . so I studied magical geometry in secret . . .*"

"*. . . tormentors tore my veil away from me, but it was I who was punished . . .*"

I listened to the bones of my sisters.

nen-sasaïr

They threw me, bruised and fettered, to my knees before the birdcage throne. I was dizzy and in pain, but this was a relief, too, after the stone-chiseled tunnels with their chalk names and their ghosts. And yet fear gnawed me. We were in the green layer of the Rainbow-Tiered Court, in a deepname-rich garden inside a lush chamber ornamented with royal swans. The birdcage was green to suit; its bars were enameled in a verdant hue, and its base and ornate crown chiseled out of malachite. Green ribbons wound from the crown of the cage, spilling gently onto the floor.

In the birdcage, the Ruler of Iyar reclined on cushions. He was dressed in robes of lustrous green, tied at the waist with a treasure of emerald. Inside this elaborate construct, he appeared stooped and hungry. Looking at me.

I had seen him, forty years ago, in this court. It had been a red day, and he had worn crimson. He was a man in his prime then, flush with his lust for more woven treasure and blood. His beard had been only barely touched by ash, his hands powerful, unwrinkled; his fingers heavy with ruby and blood-garnet rings.

The Four Profound Weaves

Such a vivid thing to remember after forty-odd years. I thought again about our lover, who died in this place. Bashri-nai-Divrah was the reason that Benesret's great weaving of song came to exist, for the Ruler of Iyar had promised us our lover's life exchanged for the greatest treasure ever woven.

"Come closer, intruder. I recognize you," said the old man in the birdcage. A studious-looking youth by the throne began to translate these words into Surun', but the Ruler of Iyar waved him down. "No need. She was born here. She can speak my language."

"It's *he*," I said. "*He* can speak your language."

The Ruler of Iyar laughed. "Yes, yes, of course. I am well aware of the temptation to play with desert-made weaves. I possess such an artifact—a cloth of winds—in fact, I collected several, even just lately. But change is not a thing I embrace. Changing my body to that of a *woman* would never occur to me. But I understand why the opposite would be tempting. Bashri-nai-Tammah."

The name fell from his lips like poison that drips from a festering wound. I knew that he spoke only to torment me, but I had to respond. "I no longer carry that name."

He waved that away. "You think me unkind, but I could have told my torturer to kill you."

The torturer stood by the Collector's side, his rod of faces intent on me. I saw in it the faces of old

131

ghosts and young; and I stared at the face of Juma, who used to be a child playing in the narrow side alleys of the outer streets of the city. IT HURTS. Juma's mouth opened wide, and within it I saw rows and rows of sharp, iron teeth. IT HURTS IT HURTS IT HURTS

I tore my eyes away from the living rod.

"In fact, since you're here," the Ruler of Iyar said briskly, "I should thank you—for delivering the Surun' weaver to me."

"Where is she?" I squeezed out. "Where is Uiziya?"

He spoke, sweet satisfaction poisoning his voice. "She is busy. So very busy."

"I have to see her."

He ignored me. "I should thank you, also, for delivering yourself to me. The men I sent to fetch you were too weak, but you helped me out. I will not make the mistake again; my torturer will make sure you are safer from now on."

"I need to see Uiziya," I repeated, stubbornly. She taught me this, my friend, the woman who never gave up. But I had left her. The brilliant green of the palace's emerald tier could not quite obstruct the truth—beneath these silks and these grasses, I sensed only death.

The Collector said, "Remember how, forty years ago, how you brought me a carpet of song? Hope, wasn't it. Hope that was made from the feathers of the goddess."

"Yes, I remember." I swallowed, for I had abandoned my questions and followed his words instead.

"What hope did you feel when you carried it, Bashri-nai-Tammah, woman of the people of the Khana?"

I turned my head away from him. From his mis-naming and mis-telling me, from his warping me out of my life. What hope did I feel then? That Bashri-nai-Divrah would live. But, in truth, as I carried the carpet that sang the melodies spun from Bird's own feathers, I dreamt even stronger of my own need, never to be called a woman again, to live in a body that matched how I knew myself to be. It would be forty years before I could finally live. For a short while.

"What hope did *you* feel," I asked the Collector, "these forty years ago, when you took the carpet of song? You hid it away."

He laughed, a croaking sound from an ancient throat. "Why, I hoped to collect even greater treasure." He looked at me, shrugged. "So many feel that there must be something more to my ambition. What more is necessary? I want things to remain, sacred and sovereign and unchanging. I want to preserve what is best. It is a noble purpose. I am not greedy for luster. I spend all my day ruling from my cage. Like the goddess Bird, who is never seen until one's final breath, I am hidden from view within these layers of stone. But I want the world to be brought to me, so I will preserve it. The landmass's truest and brightest, its art, its desire, its will, stripped of the perversions and impurities of flesh and stored away to be treasured forever. What greater ambition is needed?" He grimaced. "But I waited—you might understand it, body-changer—I waited for forty years for this carpet. I held your lover hostage while Benesret wove the treasure of song. Now I'll hold you hostage while her niece weaves from death. I am grateful to you for this balance. Balance is key."

He spoke too fast, his will was too dark for me; I could stay silent, but I did not manage. "Once it is woven—what then?"

"Oh, then?" He smiled, and I saw that some of his missing teeth were replaced by emeralds, glinting in the cavern of his hunger. "In the end I will save you. I'll honor you with a special place here, for you will have delivered to me two of the world's greatest weaves, the weaves of song and death."

I knew him, and *honor you with a special place here* was clear to me.

"You will kill me," I said.

"Yes, of course. You are a rebel—but I will treasure you."

I shook my head, unwilling to give him the satisfaction of shock or pleading. I should never have left Uiziya.

The Collector spoke still. "There is no need to deceive you. If you comply, I might preserve your companion's life."

"But you might not," I said.

"I might not. It is a risk you'll have to take; such is the nature of hope."

Hope. *Hope has been perverted here, in your Rainbow-Tiered Court, into a thing only you can possess.*

He waited for me to say something, but when I did not, he simply gestured to the torturer.

They marched me down from the green tier, down to the blue, to the indigo, to the violet, all lavishly decorated each in different style and with different patterns and art—though his best art he would have kept hidden. Beneath the violet layer was stone, rough and familiar, but unadorned. No names here.

I was pushed even lower, down even more stairs, through the vast thickness of the unliving palace. Down we descended, down to where the treasure was buried, a treasure of art from all ends of the desert and beyond, and the treasure of people who never came back.

Uiziya e Lali

I shifted, relieving the pain of sitting too still. I was not done listening to bones, but my listening acquired a lilt, a shape, a feel. I needed to make a loom from my sisters, and I needed a yarn made of them. I needed to give them a shape which the goddess Bird could not give, for she came to look for these souls and was thwarted, and then she sent mortal birds to find out what went amiss, and they all died here as well.

These bones wanted to sing—not of hope, but of something as ancient: a passing that does not yield hope, and thus is not truly a passing, for nothing changes here. Death does not guide the souls unto Bird's embrace, but returns them bereft to this place. To *his* collection.

I once—just yesterday, truly—wanted so much to please Benesret. To prove myself to her. Yet she had never truly woven a great work from death. She had made lesser weaves, garments to sell to the School of Assassins, but her greatest work had been that of hope, even though she had given it away.

Benesret said you had to care about the dead. To attempt this craft, she killed her husbands, and she killed my husband too. She was trying to teach me—knowing that you had to care deeply in order to weave from death. But she did not understand this—in her yearning, her failure, her downfall— that devouring those you cared about was not the way to this craft.

To weave from death, you had to listen to the dead. To know them deeply, to attend to what had been silenced, to care enough to help the dead speak again through every thread that made up the great work.

I needed to be alone among the bones, undisturbed, but I also needed help; and so I raised my voice and spoke in Surun'. "I heard all assassins are orphans."

The assassin kept silent.

"I heard assassins do not go with Bird when they die. Do you share a fate with these bones?"

He kept silent.

I sighed. Repeated my question. "Do you share a fate with these bones?"

"No," he said, in Surun', with the same heavy, laborious lilt I remembered. "No. The bones remain."

"And you?"

"We go into the Orphan Star, which all other stars disdained, the star that dwells under the School of Assassins. The Orphan Star alone embraces us in the end, for we have been disdained by Bird."

"It is good to die into an embrace," I said. "Would you not agree?"

He kept silent.

I spoke on, telling a story I have not often revealed. "I became an orphan when I was seven years old. I wandered the desert, wounded in my soul and helpless, and I heard the Headmaster's song and saw the light that would lead me to your school."

"But you did not reach the school," he said.

"No. I stayed with my aunt to inherit her craft. I wove from wind and made my own cloth of transformation. When the sandbirds came to me and I changed my body, the yearning to harm myself lessened, and then I could no longer hear the song." I often thought of that time as carefree, just after I changed, learning from my aunt and no longer in pain. Now I could no longer call what I felt *carefree*; but hope I had then, like never before.

"Why do you tell me this?" he asked.

"My aunt had woven from song. From all song. Even from the one that comes from the School of Assassins, for it is a form of hope."

He crossed his arms. "It is true. Those who become assassins are disdained, and they have known despair, but there is hope in the school. A hope, as you say, of being embraced in the end."

"There is hope everywhere. Even in your master's coffers."

"Not here," he said.

"Perhaps even here."

We were speechless together, two people yearning for similar things, though we served different masters. Yet I was not sure Benesret was still my master. I had waited for her and served her, but now I hesitated. She spoke and spoke about weaving from death, but all she made was these assassins' garments.

I broke the silence after a while.

"Help me make a loom from these bones. I will tell you which ones."

"I would rather not touch them," he said delicately. "Nothing must sully my garment."

I laughed, short and bitter. "What do you think your garment is made of? My aunt weaves it. It is woven from death."

The assassin looked taken aback. "The Headmaster never told us . . ."

Why would he? I shrugged. *Every master has secrets to keep. Even I do.*

He stepped closer. "Show me what needs to be done."

It took hours, but we assembled the loom from the bones of people and birds, stark and glowing now in the darkness. Beyond it, bones called and called to me: *choose me, choose me,* but some whispered, *we do not want him here,* and others whispered, *he killed us,* and yet others whispered, *first we need to be fed with living blood, for otherwise bones would never soften into a thread for your weave.*

They wanted me to kill the assassin, I knew, but I had no weapon and could not move, and he had a knife and skill that surpassed mine. I had to do the only thing I knew how: feed death with my own flesh.

"Come closer," I said to the assassin. "I saw you have a knife."

"What of it?"

"I need you to bleed me. To feed the loom."

"I . . ."

"Just me."

He came closer. "My master said to assist you." The blade glinted once more in his hand.

"Make a shallow cut then, which will bleed, but not kill."

He was close to me, taking me in, and I him. I felt a wild yearning in him, beneath all his coolness, and under it all, his bones, singing.

He opened the ample flesh of my arm where another assassin had grazed it, not so long ago. The wound that nen-sasaïr healed was open again, and blood welled from it. The assassin appeared unsettled—by my closeness, the scant light from the assembled loom, the reverie of blood. Then he took a step back, and tripped on one of the bones.

His grip on me unbalanced; my body toppled onto his. We tumbled to the ground. His arms flailed, trying to avoid my blood, which welled onto his white cloth. He twisted, desperate. And in that moment, I knew.

The fail-out we had found in Lali's tent: the diamondflies had not killed him. I had, without knowing. My blood had fallen on his cloth. And assassins must never besmirch their clothing, and they must never harm the maker of the cloth; and my aunt's blood was mine, and our spirits and lives and knowledge had mingled when I gave to her and she took from me.

The assassin began to scream and the knife fell from his fingers. My blood had burned the cloth he wore and the cloth now devoured him, consuming at first his skin. Soon it would feed on his flesh.

If he were to die in the desert, diamondflies would come to feed on the cloth and feed my aunt, but they could not find this place.

I was by his side, on the ground. Breathing hard through my pain.

"The cloth keeps you hidden and helps you kill, but you are trained never to sully it with blood, for you do not know what blood is its maker's, and so you are told to be careful in it."

He writhed on the floor, breaking the scattered bones, but the cloth had burned him, and it was too late to escape. He was being scorched to death by my blood. His body parts touched by it and the white cloth withered to nothingness. For moments, his eyes still watched me from his corroding skull, past his last breath, watched me as the rest of him withered away. I turned from him, at last. He could have been my brother. I did not wish such a death for him, but it was a death I had to give. A death which was, in some ways, less lonely, less final than the death of my sisters.

I drew on my deepnames and closed the wound he had made. This was not Benesret's wound. Just ordinary. Repairable.

"I am sorry, my friend," I told the assassin, or what remained of him. "You should hold on to this: you will go into the Orphan, unlike all these women you helped torture and kill. I simply hastened your way."

But he had no words left for me. Soon, what remained of his body corroded and fell to the floor as
fine ash; what remained of his life, of my blood, of
my aunt's cloth he wore.

Then I felt it—the vast Orphan Star, opening
wide its embrace from under the earth, from southeast and away, calling the assassin's soul home. Bird
had no access to this place, for the Ruler of Iyar had
barred it; but he had not thought to ward the place
against the Orphan.

I sighed. Perhaps in another life we were siblings.
Perhaps even in this one, for my brother had wandered away as a child, lost among the dunes. But
this man had been younger, and his Surun' speech
was different from mine.

No matter. I sighed now, and smiled, for I was
alone at last among my sisters.

nen-sasaïr

I considered my captors as they dragged me farther
below through the narrow stone corridors. The torturer was more powerful than me, even though I
had three deepnames, the most a mind could hold.
Yet his deepnames, also three, were shorter and thus
stronger than mine. He held the Warlord's Triangle,

the strongest configuration in the land. His carved iron rod was even mightier.

The second guard was not nearly as mighty. I would have expected an assassin; an assassin from the Orphan Star's school always lurked in the palace. But assassins fully trained were a precious commodity, and even the Ruler of Iyar would not have more than one. Perhaps his assassin was otherwise occupied.

"Listen," I screamed. "I have a secret to reveal to your master." I would use Benesret's words in a desperate gamble.

"Shut up," yelled the torturer, dragging me.

"The Four Profound Weaves. It is not a thing he knows—"

"We should listen," said the second guard. "Perhaps the reward—"

"Shut up!"

At last, they threw me into a cell, dark and damp, but I was satisfied, for I sensed the lingering presence of Uiziya. She'd been held somewhere close, perhaps even in this very cell, just a short time before.

The torturer said, "Now, speak your secret." In his hand, the rod of faces flushed with heat.

R. B. LEMBERG

Uiziya e Lali

I sensed nen-sasaïr in the stone above me, the familiar rattling of bones inside his flesh. I could play his bones like reed pipes, weave from them even as he lived his last breaths. He would be with me then. Not abandon me ever again.

But I was not alone, here among my dead sisters' keening. I had been abandoned through death and through dereliction, through carelessness and callous choice, through chance. But now it was my choice whether or not to abandon others.

I, an orphan, a widow, deserted and hurt by my teacher, a woman sixty-three years old—I, Uiziya e Lali, could now choose to stand by those who had been treasured here.

I lifted my hand and engaged my two deepnames, one-syllable and three-syllable, known in the desert as the Weaver's Promise, for of all crafts, our people are most given to weaves. I made of my single-syllable a central pin and spun the three-syllable around it, creating a spinning wheel of deepname light. Bone after bone I made them stretch, soft and pliant, on my spinning wheel until with my magic I spun them all into bone-thread, white from the people and deep gray and blue from the birds. And then, on my loom of bones, I wove from them all. In between the people-yarn I wove from birds, all the birds that Bird had sent to bring these women into her embrace.

But they had not died into an embrace. They died and were stagnant, unchanging, here in this chamber, killed and collected for the satisfaction of the person who ruled Iyar. I would not abandon them, and neither would they abandon me, for as I wove from them, they sang.

I wove of their death, and not of death. I wove of them, of their stories, of what remained here—smothered and stifled and dried, which the Ruler of Iyar had revealed to me only for the sake of this weaving—but all those were my sisters. They sang as I wove them, a song that begged to be heard.

nen-sasaïr

I was in the low-ceilinged stone cell that still felt like Uiziya, but she was not here. Just the torturer with his rod of faces, and his helper.

"Reveal your secret," hissed the torturer, and the faces screamed and twisted.

I had to make the most of what I had learned from Benesret. It wasn't much, but it might bring me time. Perhaps a chance.

I spoke. "The Four Profound Weaves are the greatest mystery of the desert. But I know it, and I will tell it to you. Your master said he possessed the cloth of winds. And then Uiziya's sand-woven carpet; and her aunt Benesret's great carpet of song. Soon he will have the last of them, which is woven from death. The secret is what happens when those four are put together."

The torturer swung the flaming rod into the flesh of my side, and I screamed unreservedly, endlessly. I put all my power into the scream, and as I did so, on the very edge of my voice, I heard music.

"What is the secret?" the torturer shouted, as persistent as Uiziya.

"I don't know," I lied. "I don't know!"

He hit me again, the rod twisting into my flesh.

"The secret of the sibling gods," I screamed at last, as in my mind the holy music swelled and stung. *It is simple—the sibling gods would come closer if the four are put together, summoned by the desert's deepest weaves.*

I did not speak this, but what I said was enough.

The torturer snapped at the guard, "Go. Tell this to the master." When the guard hesitated, the torturer snarled, "Go! I will manage."

We were alone.

He said, "If you think you will escape, think again. I see you have three deepnames. Your Builder's Triangle might be great for artifice, but it is no match for my Warlord's Triangle, let alone my rod."

I had brought myself time, but I did not understand how to resist him, and despair flooded my already painful and weary body. I called on my deepnames, the one syllable, two syllables, three syllables, to create a healing weave, to lessen at least the pain in the flesh, but the torturer sensed my intent. He laughed, and shoved the hungry faces into my flesh once again. I saw the child up close, his rows of sharp, iron teeth opening to consume me. He, too, was beloved once, and was still beloved.

As I thought this, the edges of my healing magic stirred toward Juma. I did not resist the impulse, and my power washed gently over his face. The child stopped screaming and looked at me, and the other faces twisted around, their mouths opening and closing, while I stared down at them.

None of this the torturer noticed. "You have such powerful deepnames. I should tear them away from your mind. I hear that you were born a woman, and women should not carry deepnames." He shoved me again with the rod. As he did so, the faces screamed in pain once more. I felt my mind tear as the teeth grasped my flesh, and the torturer's magic closed on my two-syllable deepname, like a vise. Why this one, I did not know. It was the most active in working the healing, but now it stretched under the onslaught of the torturer's power. I screamed, flailing, and even as I screamed, I saw the child's face in the rod as it twisted away from me.

It did not bite.

Because I had eased his pain.

"Juma," I mouthed, my pain overwhelming, fighting to keep my eyes focused on the child's face. "Your friend worried for you—Juma—"

The child's mouth closed, and their eyes bulged. The women in the rod, too, unlatched their teeth from my flesh and turned their faces towards me. They were Juma's mother and grandmothers, grandfather, uncle. The torturer's loved ones whose deepnames and then lives he had taken to serve him.

The torturer's power still was latched on to my two-syllable deepname, and then, through the pain, at the very edge of my senses, I heard again the holy song. I thought I had left it behind when I turned away from the lock and from the white walls of the Khana men's domain. I thought I had fled the voice of my god. But Kimri was right here, had always been here, listening to all my screams and my silences. The hidden god waited for me to sing.

But I could not sing yet. With a terrible sound in my mind, my two-syllable *snapped*, and my ears filled with a terrible noise. The torturer tried to burn the deepname out, but in the tug and struggle between us, the name was not dead, just broken. It was longer and weaker now, a three-syllable where a two-syllable had once been.

I swayed on my feet. Pain twisted and burned me, but the noise in my ears receded and the holy song flowed in me once again, supporting me. I looked inward now. Healing magic was difficult and imprecise, and I had failed to heal Uiziya, but I heard it said that delicate healings were easier with long names. Shaking, I made a new healing structure with my weak three-syllable deepnames: one of them whole and afraid, the other broken, struggling, longer than it was before, but alive. Gritting my teeth, I directed my will at the twisting rod.

Then I spoke to the faces in the iron, an echo of the god's melody in my mind.

"Silent or screaming, I hear you. I see you. Juma—oh Juma—song is forever only a breath away. Do not be afraid to be heard—yes, even in your death—for if your voice is heard, it is no longer possible to pretend that you do not exist."

"What are you saying—?" In the torturer's hand the rod twisted, each face straining to open its mouth.

One by one, the faces began to sing, the song of rage and heat and blood overflowing with the voices of the torturer's victims, his loved ones twisting in unbearable pain of their love. The torturer shook his hand, frantic to get the weapon away from him.

At this moment I aimed my painful, exultant, weaker and yet more deliberate magic. I wrapped the twisting, roaring, singing rod in my structure of deepnames and drove it up, into the torturer's eye, through his skull.

He fell down. Slowly, I spun my magic once more and destroyed the lock. My power was no match for the torturer's, but I knew mechanical things.

I stepped out, stealing furtive glances upon the

body, the still-twitching rod. I told myself to take the rod, but I was terrified, even though I had healed it.

My head felt splitting with pain. I could no longer hold my magical structure. Kimri's song steered me away, out of these chambers, and down the stairs, farther below, toward Uiziya e Lali.

Uiziya e Lali

I heard the rattling of flesh-encased bones beyond the door. Nen-sasaïr. I ignored him.

I had finished my weave. The Ruler of Iyar would come for me, to take the carpet I had made, and to kill me. Until then, I did not want to move.

On my loom, the finished piece glittered, a tapestry of hurts that wept and screamed and cursed and blessed and fell silent, exhausted, before taking up speech again. My great tapestry of death, Benesret's dream, which was now my work.

The lock clicked, and clicked again, and flew open at last.

I spoke. "Cease your steps and come no further, for it is not a place for men."

Nen-sasaïr ignored me. Stepped over the threshold. Walked closer.

He looked wounded and yet buoyant, as if some

echo of song held him up. His bloodshot eyes were on the loom. He looked at the great work I had made, the ornamentation I had created from all those slain here—the white weave of the bone-thread; the pale gray shapes of birds; a red slash of horizon swelling with dawn.

"Step no further," I warned him. "For I had woven from death, and only death lies this way."

"I must. I will. It is my lover you have woven from."

One voice separated itself from the threads and sang in nen-sasaïr's language.

nen-sasaïr

"Forty years."

I shuddered, hearing it. Hearing her—the lilt of her voice, that little breath she took at the end of each sentence. She had been young still, Bashri-nai-Divrah; barely twenty when she died in this place.

My own voice, bounded with years, tired, lower than ever she heard it, was old. Old and pleading. "We brought the carpet to buy your life back, but you were already dead."

"He tricked you, you know. He needed your ardor to bring back the carpet."

Yes, I'd realized that, years ago. He had lured

Bashri-nai-Divrah in on purpose; the treacherous trade had been no accident.

"I am so, so sorry," I told her, words that I yearned for forty years to say. "I am sorry for your death. For your imprisonment here, even after you died. I am sorry for us. For the years. I am sorry."

The tapestry sang with her voice. *"And have you found solace in the years?"*

"Yes." I said, "When I went back to find Benesret. I transformed my body."

I did not know what I wanted her to say. *I always knew. How could you do this, go against the law? I still love you: a man, a woman, I would always love you. I'd be with you, if I could live.*

But what she sang was, *"Where is Bashri?"*

The question staggered me, burned me worse than the torturer's rod of faces. I had been called Bashri, and so was Bashri-nai-Divrah, but *Bashri* was always and ever Bashri-nai-Leylit. We two others took her name when we formed our oreg, our trading-group, our family, our lovers'-group. Bashri-nai-Leylit, who did not want me to change, who kept my cloth of winds in her strongbox until she died—this was the question asked now by my other lover, even from beyond death.

I said bitterly, "Bashri-nai-Leylit was carried aloft by a dove. In her old age."

I do not know what I wanted to hear. *I am sorry,* perhaps. Or *Did she speak of me before she died?*

The tapestry sang instead, *"Was she happy?"*

It was a tapestry, and it was my lover. The other Bashri. Bashri-nai-Divrah.

"No," I said. "We were not happy. My secret burdened her and bent her, until she could hold it no more. And I could hold it no more. So I traveled to find my Surun' friends, and transformed my body, even though I am old."

The carpet spoke, but no longer in the voice of Bashri-nai-Divrah alone. I heard many voices together. Some sounded ancient and some were new; some were Khana, most were Iyari, and some I could not understand at all. I could not distinguish among them; the voices were threads, each separate and yet woven tightly together. The carpet of death spoke to me.

"The Ruler of Iyar keeps secrets—"

"He keeps us, and all those works of our hands, of our splendor, locked forever—"

"It is wrong to make a treasure of another, however tenderly kept—"

"There is no right or wrong here. Only bones."

The tapestry fell silent.

Uiziya said, "He will send someone to fetch my carpet, if you want to wait here with me."

I did not want to remain there. The carpet of death sang and beckoned, drawing my soul in to join in the weave. The darkness around it was complete. I had lived long enough; wasn't it better to be woven with my dead lover, to sing forever like I had wanted to sing?

We could perhaps find him on our own, the Ruler of Iyar, wandering through the corridors. Uiziya could not walk, and I wasn't strong enough to support her well. The moving chair I had made was destroyed, and Uiziya's carpet of wanderlust had been taken.

"I will stay," I said.

We waited, together, in the dark by the carpet of death.

Uiziya e Lali

We did not have to wait long for guards to arrive. They looked terrified of the place that now gaped cavernous and hungry, emptied of bones. The guards poked and prodded at nen-sasaïr, but they brought me a cane and allowed him to support me. I carried the carpet of death over my shoulder; the guards would not touch it, and would not touch me, and maybe because of that they wanted both us alive.

The Ruler of Iyar waited for us in a chamber of stone full of armored chests that stood open, overflowing with all manner of treasure—tapestries and carpets, small rugs of bird feathers made in the Mon

Mountain fashion, spidersilk sashes embroidered with gold. His birdcage stood open and empty; the enjoyment of his treasures required him to step outside it. He was attended by three new people who had replaced his torturer, his physicker, and his assassin.

When the guards brought us in, he was not surprised to see both of us together.

"What happened to my assassin and my torturer? Never mind. People always disappoint you," he said. "Yet I am their anchor, their center, their core."

"Those who have forsaken you are dead," I said. "You killed many of them yourself, remember?"

"Isn't it the same? You yourself were forsaken, and so you have woven from death. As you have woven from death, so I wish to preserve my subjects, to shelter them, treasure them. My torturer imitated me, you know. A pupil always tries to follow his master. Just as you followed Benesret."

No. Not like I followed Benesret.

But the Collector spoke on. "He killed his family, even his child, to be treasured within the rod. I thought that ingenious, until he, too, deserted me. People disappoint you. Treasures alone will never forsake or betray you."

I saw now the weavings spread at his feet.

The multicolored cloth of winds felt new. Made by a skilled yet young weaver, it scintillated with all the promise of joy, of dawns and of butterflies; a few of the small pink ones fluttered up from the weave. I had seen this cloth of winds before, just before we left the encampment—woven by Kimi, nen-sasaïr's youngest grandchild. Next to the wind-cloth, my own old and tattered carpet of sand appeared restless, shivering on the floor as if ready to fly away.

Last was that great and intricate weave of blue and emerald green that I remembered from my youth; I had stood by my aunt's loom to witness its weaving. Zurya of the Maiva'at had sung the singing thread from Bird's own feathers until it choked her. My aunt had woven from that pain, and the glory of Bird-song, and from her own yearning. Benesret's greatest hope—to weave from death, but her greatest weave, in the end, was hope.

The Ruler of Iyar said, "I see the carpet of death in your hands. You have completed it. Brought it to me. Now spread it at my feet, with the others."

He motioned to his guards, and they forced both of us down, nen-sasaïr to his knees, me down by his side. Together we spread my tapestry at his feet, by the carpet of song.

The Ruler of Iyar smiled down at us, at my pain. Then he stepped on the carpet of wind. His feet crushed the fluttering butterflies, and nen-sasaïr cried at my side. The Ruler of Iyar had taken his lover away, just as now he stepped on his grandchild's great joy.

"Change is a lie," said the Ruler of Iyar to nen-sasaïr. "You tried to change so much, you ran away to the desert, but you ended back here."

The Ruler of Iyar stepped next on the carpet of sand, and I cried out, for he was walking on me. "All your yearning and wanderlust had come to nothing. You journeyed only for my purpose." And it was true—I came here from the snake-Surun' encampment, to weave for him at his command, from these bones he had made.

He stepped on the great carpet of song, and there was a great outcry from it, a scream of a wounded bird, for it was upon the goddess's own feathers that he was stepping now, and it tore me apart. "Hope is always the easiest to defeat," he said. "You gave it up to me, yourselves."

I found no words to defy him, and neither did nen-sasaïr.

"Now," the Ruler of Iyar said, "The four weaves are together. The secret of the gods, as you said."

He stepped on the carpet of death. On my sisters.

nen-sasaïr

He stepped on the carpet of death, and as he did, the song I kept hearing since I had touched the lock in the Khana quarter began to surge in me, filling my broken, painful mind, filling all the empty silent spaces behind my eyes, in my throat.

"The secret of the gods," said the Ruler of Iyar. "What is it? I'm waiting. Or have you lied?"

I spoke. "With the weave of sand and wind supporting them, the weave of death will bring Bird closer, for she comes for the dead in her many forms; and the weave of song will bring forth her brother, the singer, Kimri."

The Ruler of Iyar frowned. "Is that all?"

I took a deep breath, and opened my mouth once again.

"Bird's feathers made the threads that Benesret wove into her great carpet of song; and the bone-threads Uiziya had made from the women you killed will now sing. Hope and death; the siblings are intertwined, and this is the mystery of the ever-changing desert. Hope cannot be given away, to you, or to anyone. Hope is the song which arises from silence where all our voices had been; all those locked away against their will one day will surge again, come forth with great exuberance, sweep the world in a reverberation of rainbow more true than your Rainbow-Tiered Court."

I noticed now that I had been singing; I sang all those words that came through me, out of me, and the weavings of death and of hope joined me now, bringing closer the goddess and the god, the siblings, into this place. "Because the dawn is never far away."

And then I sang and sang, not seeing anything anymore, for the god had brought me my name.

My throat hoarse from effort and silent at last, I opened my eyes and saw them all on their knees—not just the two of us, but the Ruler's guards, and the Ruler of Iyar himself, shielding his ears in vain against the triumphant music. The siblings were intertwined: Bird's brother contained all the world's dead, brought to him by his sister Bird, but he did not take them. The song did not have the power to kill, only to sway and strain and wound and heal the hearts of those who heard it.

I looked at the faces around me. Uiziya. The guards. The Ruler of Iyar. Ecstatic, remorseful, defiant.

Uiziya's hands stretched out, as if in supplication, toward the tapestry she had woven from bones. The Ruler of Iyar screamed at her, against the surging of the song, "They are mine! All mine! I preserve them! All mine!"

She tugged on the carpet made of all the dead women he'd killed and hidden. The motion unbalanced her, and I saw the pain in her face as she pulled and pulled on the carpet. Screaming with the exhaustion of her body, screaming her anguish, her defiance, she lifted it up and threw it.

The carpet of death wrapped around the Ruler's head. His shoulders. His arms. And it fed.

AFTERWEAVE

Uiziya e Lali

Leaving the palace, I was shaking with exhaustion and overcome by the body's pain, but nen-sasaïr supported me. He found a plain staff, a cane I could lean on, and he draped it with my carpet of sand. Its magic helped me move. Nen-sasaïr found another cane for himself too—he was shaken and hurt, though it was nothing I could see. Still, he carried the carpets of wind and song. I carried the carpet of death slung over my shoulder; I held on to my new staff with the other hand. It was a precarious balance, but nobody else would touch the white carpet, not even nen-sasaïr.

That fear was a helper to us; in the confusion of the Collector's demise, the palace guards would neither touch nor hinder us, their eyes wide at the whispering carpet of death, then shying away. Perhaps they were secretly relieved that the Collector was dead, but I thought it more likely that they wanted to avoid his death and its weaver. And so we escaped.

Dawn was breaking over the springflower city of Iyar, and from the rooftops of the palace, a plaintive sound of a reed pipe could be heard. I expected something grander—the wailing of wind-pipes from all the roofs of the city, a great tumult of people—but perhaps that would come later. I would have to sleep soon, but it was not safe yet to do so, and so we pushed through. The carpet of song that nen-sasaïr carried revived us just enough to make it to the gate.

Juma's friend waited for us there, a small child of eleven or twelve, an in-betweener called Riát. Nen-sasaïr talked to them. I was barely awake by then. Something about the rod.

"I could not touch it," nen-sasaïr said. "I was afraid to pick it up. It is still somewhere in the palace, in the dungeons, but we were too exhausted to go look for it—my magic was broken—I'm sorry—"

"I guess you cannot help being old," said the child. And to me, "Is it true that your carpet ate the Collector?"

"The souls of those he harmed devoured him," I said.

"Just like the rod devoured Juma's dad."

"She does not know about the torturer," nen-sasaïr said. "I am sorry we could not do more."

"You have done enough." The child looked up

and west, in the direction of the palace. "Perhaps the name-orphans of Iyar can collect what is ours."

"Be careful," said nen-sasaïr.

"Get some sleep," said the child.

But we could not sleep in the city. Once out of the gates, we made my carpet of sand fly again. Not too far away, we found a small, fertile valley, and an orchard of plums, and there we slept for three days. I guess we really could not help being wounded and old, but the plums and the sleep did their work. Nen-sasaïr's head did not hurt as much anymore, though he still complained that he heard, when he was tired, either terrible noise or the holy song, and he wasn't sure how to combine his new deepnames.

"This configuration, I do not even know what it is called. It does not feel stable." But he tried, again and again, to use it; it did not work nearly as well as before, but his healing improved, and he eased my pain, if not his own.

After resting some more, we flew southeast, leaving behind Iyar's lush orchards and fields, toward where the sand greets the sky.

We journeyed for days until at last we found Benesret's encampment of bones on a different outcropping of rock; while we traveled, she had migrated south. In the light of mid-morning, the skulls and bones looked almost pacified, pressed down under the growing weight of the sun.

I let the carpet of sand touch ground, and nen-sasaïr helped me stand. I supported myself on my cane. The pain of my withered leg was familiar now, and duller, just another insistent part of the song of pain that my body made.

Benesret looked startled to see us. A little alarmed. When nen-sasaïr gave her the carpet of song, she hardly looked at it.

"I took your flesh," she said to me. "And still you came back."

If she thought we would kill her, she was mistaken. We had brought her the carpet, and now I wanted to talk.

"You could have taken anyone," I said. "Shrubs growing furtively in the desert's heat, lizards darting around, sandplovers with their curved beaks; you could have stepped between worlds, taken the razu beast in flight. You could have created living beings with your great mastery of the weaving arts. You could have created them and taken them." Nen-sasaïr shuddered, hearing my words. I pressed on. "But you have taken *me*."

"You asked me."

"Because I wanted you to teach me."

"The weave of death must be made from those you care about. I told you this, but you would not attend. I killed your husband," Benesret said. "Took his life, drop by leeched drop for my work. Grief upon grief you have known—but still it wasn't enough for you to truly desire to weave from death.

You were content to remain in the leather tents with your children and your nieces and your goats, forever yearning for my instruction yet never seeking me out, never weaving anything of magic until you followed *him* here. Until you asked me."

"Until you *harmed* me." I wondered now why she had not taken my children.

Benesret said, "You should be grateful, for it is because I took you that you have learned this, and wove at last from death."

Benesret's eyes shone with hunger as she looked at the bone-white tapestry I had tucked under my arm. With nen-sasaïr's help I spread it for her now, bone and ash and yearning and song.

See? I wanted to say. *I, a weaver who spent forty years in the tents, discontent yet unmoved even in grief, I, a mortal who would not even learn from you, I have surpassed you.* I was tempted to say that, but it was not right. Craft she had aplenty, and between the two of us, she was the greater weaver still. The carpet of song reverberated with a great precision, her mastery, but she did not want what she'd woven. What she wanted was the work I had done.

"You devoured all these people, devoured even me, because you must care for the people you take for your work." I'd seen this in her—and in the torturer, whose family he killed to create the rod. I saw this even in the Ruler of Iyar. "I have learned this: that you can care about the dead without devouring them. Without using them. This is my story, and my weave."

"I do not know how to do this," she said. And yet she was alive, when both the torturer and the Collector had died. There was a reason for that.

"You sought out death as your craft, Aunt," I said, "but your greatest weaving was hope. Hope and death are intertwined, inseparable like the sibling gods. That is the secret of the Four Profound Weaves."

"There is no more hope for me," Benesret said, her voice ragged. "And even if there was, Bird would never take me up. Not after all of this. Never. All I ever wanted was to make the great last weave; but you have surpassed me."

"This is not about ambition or craft." I had never aspired to this. "In the darkest place that even Bird could not find, I wove from my sisters. If you care about someone strongly enough, if you listen hard to their stories, perhaps one day you will find yourself in that place."

We left Benesret with her carpet of song, and journeyed farther into the desert.

nen-sasaïr

We traveled southeast until we found a great out-cropping of rock shimmering with indigo and the rainbow of mineral salt. We had been looking for this place or one much like it, a place we had never visited but that had called to us from afar. It was hot and bright, and our eyes swam from heat and sweat. The carpet of sand floated to the ground. Struggling, de-termined, we lifted the tapestry of death, the greatest treasure ever woven, and offered it to the sky.

For many long moments, the tilting world of the desert was silent. Then, one by one, the threads began to sing. Not as triumphantly as the carpet of song had sung, not as grandly, but it made the air melt in my lungs with the redness of heat, with the swelling of yearning. In all their languages the dead sang, in Iyari and Khanishti and Burrashti and Surun', and other languages I did not know. No more did the dead sing their lives; instead they sang this light, the wide-open spaces, the scorching sun-glare, the wind.

My eyes ran with tears, so at first all I saw was a blur tumbling down from the sun. I thought that it was a sandbird, like the birds that came to me during my ritual of transformation. But it was no sandbird. It was the goddess herself.

Bird came in the shape of a great swan of bone, her skeletal wings spread wide and her long neck curving. The swan wasn't a desert bird, but a sigil of royal Iyar, stripped now of flesh and feather.

Her empty eye sockets looked into my soul. The great beak tugged at the tapestry.

We let it go into Bird's keeping, and she carried it up just a bit. And then she began to dance.

Bones, bones, oh how her bones rattled above the swirling sun-domain of the desert, rattling like drums, like the first and last music that ever existed. In her beak, Uiziya's great weaving shook and dissolved into ash. Floating, swirling over our heads so that even the sun was obscured. Then a strong gust of wind bore ash and Bird away. The heat filled the world once more.

I stood there, bereft and teetering, next to Uiziya. At last, I wiped my eyes with the sleeve of my garment. "What does it mean?" But I knew what it meant; that for all our endeavor, Bird would not take up the souls of our dead.

"I think it means," said Uiziya, "that some wrongs can never be fully remedied even by the gods, no matter how great our effort. But the wind and the sand will remember."

The wind, shifting my lover's ash, all the lost women's ash, all around the great desert. The wind, traveling through all lands that ever existed, mingling ash with sand, weaving the desert out of our yearning, our wanderlust, so the desert itself may wander, so it may change and remember itself anew in the voices of the never-born and the dead, making out of itself pasts and futures in which all is possible.

And from afar, I heard the echo of my lover's voice.

"*Remember me—a woman of the people of the Khana, a lover of Bashri-nai-Leylit and of the one whose true name became . . .*"

I whispered, "Kaveh-nen-Kimri," for it was the name given to me by my god. Kaveh: a man who has hope.

"*. . . and of Kaveh-nen-Kimri, a man of the people of the Khana and my lover, whose story is woven into the great weave of the land.*"

The sound of Bashri-nai-Divrah's voice was almost palpable, sand-gold and warm and then fading into silver, folded into the retreating wind.

It was done. I wanted it to be done differently. I wanted the woman I loved at the dawn of my life to be back, this woman I hardly knew; and I wanted Bashri-nai-Leylit, who wept now, above, wrapped in the dove-wings of the goddess. I wanted a story that ended in hope, but all I could see, as far as I looked, was ash.

Uiziya e Lali

"Do not look so forlorn," I said to Kaveh. "Our work was not for nothing. This wind and these sands are a life beyond death, unlike the stone-cold prisons of Iyar."

I felt his grip tighten on my arm, steadying me. "I think it is true, and yet I fear. Soon a new ruler will rise in Iyar, and he again will collect treasure."

"I understand this fear." I had shaped from death, but I was not burdened by it, for the bone-tapestry I had made was created from the song's defiance, too. Here under the open skies where the ash of my sisters was woven now into the desert, I felt a new feeling expand my chest.

"Yes," I said, "A new ruler will rise in Iyar, to do this and worse, unspeakable things until the world overflows with them, and the scream of the bones chokes the land. But this I know: new weavers will rise among our peoples, new weavers who will raise their voices even if that music is made of their bones; and these new makers will weave and be woven, from hope and death, to bring the collector down. Over and over will we rise."

Kaveh said, "That is hope."

"No," I said. "More than hope. It is the truth of the weaves, as profound as the wind and the sand and the certainty of death."

Kaveh-nen-Kimri

I stood listening for all my lost lovers and for Bird until my head felt like it would split with the heat, and my eyes refused to see anymore.

Uiziya touched my sleeve. "Where will you go now?"

My hand touched my chin, where the stubble of a gray and black beard was growing unshaved for the first time. I was a Khana man and I was perhaps expected to answer *home*. Home, to the lock of song in the Khana quarter, where Kimri was waiting for me for the first time, my god, to let me into the smallest of places from which a song issues forth. But I had turned away from that life, and still Kimri came to me. Song was everywhere. I did not have to go anywhere to find him. Perhaps one day I would return, but I was a man who was brought up a woman of the Khana, and I had the love of trade routes and wide-open spaces. *Home* ran between my fingers like ash, and was carried away by the wind.

Yet I did not speak.

I wanted to be as sure as Uiziya, but I was not sure of anything—of what we had wrought, my lover's words within the ash, the nature of the weaves, the certainty of hope's resilience, which is as strong as the certainty of death. But I had to tell this tale to my grandchildren. For we are all woven of words; and after we go, it is our tales that remain, wandering around the desert with the wind until our stories are told four times, until a weave is pulled from them— the carpet of truth which is this desert, this weave of change, and wanderlust, and hope, and death.

Uiziya e Lali

"Where will you go?" I asked again, for I was stubborn and would keep asking until I was satisfied.
I saw him smile, at last—just a small tugging of the lips, but I knew him: Kaveh-nen-Kimri, a man of the people of the Khana. My friend.

"I am going back to the snake-Surun' encampment, to my grandchildren, to return the carpet of wind to Kimi, and to tell the story. Then—away. I might be old, but I'm not ready yet to be done. I want to learn more about my new magic. I want see what lies beyond—to the east, where the sacred tumbleweed wanders, a star in its heart; and beyond, where youths send their mountain hawks up to greet the dawn. I lost my sand-skis, and I would need to find a workshop and make myself new ones—if I even can now—but perhaps we can use your carpet of wanderlust, if you want to come with me."

"My old carpet? Hah. Not this thing." It was good to be sure at last both of myself and my craft. "I will weave you one better."

My friend surveyed the horizon, as if looking out for a way ahead. He adopted my way in the end, and repeated his question, more tentatively than I would ask it. "Would you come with me?"

I did not hesitate. "Of course I will."

ACKNOWLEDGMENTS

This book would not have been possible without editors who, over the course of years, took chances on my works set in Birdverse, and works that formed the great weave of this story. Amal El-Mohtar and Jessica Wick published my poem about the making of the greatest treasure ever woven, which went on to place in the Rhysling Award. One of my greatest lessons and gifts in this life is learning to move aside so the words can come through, and this poem paved the way. I wrote "Grandmother-nai-Leylit's Cloth of Winds" next. It was a novelette, and I am grateful to my editor Scott H. Andrews for publishing it in *Beneath Ceaseless Skies*. That piece was a finalist for the Nebula Award, and for that I am forever grateful to my readers who voted for it, discussed it, believed in it, argued with it. "Cloth" is a story of a family—a story of the trans and non-binary members of that family, as told by a queer cisgender relative, Aviya. It wasn't the most comfortable viewpoint for me as a non-binary person, but it allowed me to say things about queer and trans family dynamics that I needed to say at that point in my life. A few years later, I wrote *The Four Profound Weaves*. It is a work that came to me after my father's death. For a short, painful time after he passed, I thought I was done writing. This was the work that came after. It seems that I was not done writing about families, or about this particular family, but the trans viewpoints were the ones I was going to foreground. I am grateful to the crew at Tachyon, and especially to my editor Jaymee Goh, who did a fantastic job helping me develop a much shorter and shallower draft into the book you are reading now. Jaymee's attention to detail, deep understanding of LGBTQIA+ issues in storytelling, and most excellent sense of humor made working on edits a pleasure. Jill Roberts, the managing editor at Tachyon, helped me take the book even further by suggesting ways to develop the story and its characters. Special thanks to Jacob Weisman at Tachyon, and to my former agent Connor Goldsmith, for making the book a reality. Many thanks to early readers Corey Alexander, Elora Gatts, Sonya Taaffe, Bryn Greenwood, Jay Wolf, and to my sensitivity reader Izzy Wasserstein, for their insights and support. Much gratitude to my wonderful Patreon supporters, who followed along as I developed and edited this book. I could not have written this book without the encouragement, support, invaluable suggestions, and anti-brain-weasel efforts of my spouse, Bogi Takács. Our child Mati contributed hugs and excitement regardless of whether or not I wrote anything. Last but not least, I am grateful to the splendid fellowship of queer and trans writers in my online writing group, to whom this book is dedicated.

ABOUT THE AUTHOR

R.B. Lemberg is a queer, bigender immigrant from Eastern Europe and Israel. Their stories and poems have appeared in *Lightspeed Magazine's Queers Destroy Science Fiction!, Beneath Ceaseless Skies, Uncanny Magazine, Sisters of the Revolution: A Feminist Speculative Fiction Anthology*, and many other venues. R.B.'s work has been a finalist for the Nebula, Crawford, and other awards. You can find more of their work on their Patreon (patreon.com/rblemberg) and a full bio at rblemberg.net